"I didn't get asked out a single time in high school."

"Oh, please. A girl as beautiful as you didn't date?"

"My looks were just one more strike against me. The girls were jealous, so they never included me, and the boys figured they wouldn't have a chance, so they didn't bother asking."

Luke stopped walking and stared down into her questioning eyes. "Well, this boy's gonna bother. Claire Savage, will you have dinner with me?"

"Are you asking me on a *date*?"

"Well, no—you don't have to sound so shocked by the possibility. Friends do occasionally spend time together, you know."

She stood on tiptoe and kissed his cheek. "Thanks for asking. Sure, I'll go to dinner with you…friend."

But before her heels could even touch the ground, he brought his lips down to meet hers....

Books by Mae Nunn

Love Inspired

Hearts in Bloom #254
*Sealed with a Kiss #293
*Amazing Love #336

*Texas Treasures

MAE NUNN

grew up in Houston and graduated from the University of Texas with a degree in communications. When she fell for a transplanted Englishman who lived in Atlanta, Mae hung up her spurs to become a Southern belle. Today, she and her husband, Michael, and their two children make their home in Georgia. Mae has been with a global air express company for twenty-seven years, currently serving as a Director of Specialty Services. She began writing four years ago. When asked how she felt about being part of the Steeple Hill family, Mae summed her response up with one word—"Yeeeeeha!"

AMAZING LOVE

MAE NUNN

Steeple
Hill®

Published by Steeple Hill Books™

Dedication
This book is for Sunny.
7/28/49–1/1/05

STEEPLE HILL BOOKS

Steeple
Hill®

ISBN 0-373-87350-6

AMAZING LOVE

Copyright © 2006 by Mae Nunn

This edition published by arrangement with Steeple Hill Books.

® and TM are trademarks of Steeple Hill Books, used under license. Trademarks indicated with ® are registered in the United States Patent and Trademark Office, the Canadian Trade Marks Office and in other countries.

www.SteepleHill.com

Printed in U.S.A.

Blessed is he whose transgressions are forgiven,
whose sins are covered. Blessed is the man whose
sin the Lord does not count against him
and in whose spirit is no deceit.

—*Psalms* 32:1–2

Acknowledgments

I owe my gratitude to so many who impacted this project, whether they knew it or not.

To my Crossroads Church family in Newnan, Georgia, (especially the Williams/Worhola/Zauner Community Group) where "Being and Building Disciples of Christ" is a way of life.

To the readers who gave me so much positive feedback on *Hearts in Bloom* and encouraged me to take the faith in my writing to a deeper level.

To my daughter, Maegan, my sunshine.

To my son, Paul, for planting a seed that grew into the character of Luke Dawson.

To my darlin' Michael—
you make it all worthwhile.

And to three incredible women who prove it's never too late to become biker babes. My amazing sister Pam Hruza has never let me down, not even once. My gifted critique partner, Silhouette author Dianna Love Snell, makes me a better writer. And my precious friend Sunny Rigsby inspired me with her "Ride it like you stole it!" enthusiasm for life.

Chapter One

Claire Savage gripped the wooden knob of the stick shift and dropped the limited-edition pink pony into low gear for the steep climb up the bridge that spanned the Houston ship channel. On a Saturday morning when the worst driving hazard should have been glare from the relentless Texas summer sun, something just beyond the crest of the high, arching bridge interrupted the progress of weekend traffic.

As a chain reaction of red taillights flashed, she jammed a foot on the brake of her 1967 coupe. Her gaze flew to the rearview mirror and she pleaded aloud with the truck on her tail not to collide with the recently rechromed bumper. The driver struggled but managed to control his heavy-duty pickup and the fully rigged boat that fishtailed behind him. Within moments, everything ground to a standstill.

Claire switched off the finicky air conditioner

and cranked the window down. She pumped the clutch with her left foot and accelerated with her right as the traffic crept forward, inching up the sharp incline along with the other vehicles. Rubberneckers turned their heads to catch a glimpse of the nuisance that dared to delay their interstate progress.

Curious like everybody else, she sat tall in the seat and craned her neck to see beyond the sedan in front. When a long-legged, yellow Lab pup lumbered between the cars up ahead, her hand flew to her face to cover the gasp that escaped her mouth.

Horns blared and the bewildered animal darted in one direction, then another. Panic ballooned in Claire's chest for the poor dog that was surely moments from tragedy. She punched the emergency flashers, shifted the manual transmission into neutral and pulled the hand brake. As she reached for the door handle, another flash of movement caught her eye.

A male figure in faded jeans and a black T-shirt wove between the vehicles, alternately appealing to the dog and then waving thanks to the drivers for their patience. The scene was as charming and heroic as it was dangerous and foolhardy.

Who was she calling foolhardy?

Her hand was still poised to push the door open so she could call the dog to safety herself. Beaten to the punch, she breathed a sigh of relief.

Three foster pets at one time were enough. She needed to find permanent homes for Buck, Tripod and R.C. before she took in any more animals.

God's grace was clearly with the Good Samaritan as the otherwise aggressive Houston drivers became amazingly cooperative with the rescue attempt. Claire's heart melted over the loving way he coaxed the terrified Lab, now paralyzed with fear.

"Come here, buddy," the man urged, as he crept closer. "It's okay, Luke's gonna take good care of you."

Shuddering from head to tail, the pup cowered on the hot pavement and hung his chin. He flinched the moment a gentle hand made contact with his dirty coat, but then lifted huge, pleading eyes in gratitude. The man squatted, scooped the dog into his long arms and held it securely to his chest.

Claire swallowed the lump in her throat, thinking of the lost sheep parable. But the thought was immediately erased when the man turned about-face to carry the dog away from the traffic. She was glad for the dark shades over her wide eyes as she studied him.

Where his face was Bruce Willis attractive, the flesh on the left side of his neck, from his jawbone to the collar of his shirt, bore an angry scar.

She sucked in her breath, ashamed to be staring.

"Thanks, everybody," he called but seemed to avoid any particular eye contact.

"God bless you for what you just did," she said aloud, though he was out of earshot.

As traffic began to inch forward, she kept an eye on his progress until he made it to the side of the bridge, where she lost sight of him.

Savage Cycles was only minutes away as the crow flies, but the drive seemed much longer with the memory of the rescue scene on constant replay. Claire viewed the mental picture of the man in black from every angle. The close-cropped dark hair and clean-shaven jaw packed a masculine punch. The muscular arms that embraced the pup belied the gentle nature of the stranger. The long legs encased in denim gave him a casual air. The ruddy scar tissue.

An unforgettable image.

Arriving at her destination, she found the parking lot of Savage Cycles already a hub of activity. It was no surprise since most serious bikers were gearing up for the annual Black Hills Rally. The regulars lived for these weekend get-togethers at her dealership, giving it a constant party atmosphere.

That was just one of the reasons she had been determined to become a partner, after observing the thrilling and unfamiliar sport of motorcycling as Sam Kennesaw's business manager. When the former owner married and moved back to East Texas to resume his teaching career, Sam sold his pride and joy to Claire. She'd come to love this wild business, as he had. Now the hectic job was her sanctuary from the painful nightmare that couldn't be counseled away, the memory of the abuse that couldn't be buried deeply enough.

She thrived on the fact that every chopper sale was a new challenge, each customer a unique discovery about human nature. The sport offered a never-ending supply of interesting characters who were more concerned with her knowledge of product and finance than her personal history, physical features or local celebrity.

"Good morning, Claire," Justin called from behind the counter.

She waved a greeting to her parts manager and the leather-clad customer being assisted. En route to her office she stopped to survey the showroom with a critical glance. A half-dozen new bikes were angled before the windows, beckoning to passersby.

Angled the wrong way.

She ground her teeth.

The employees had followed her instructions without question when she'd managed the business for Sam. After signing the papers and taking control, she'd overlooked the occasional incident when someone would "do it the old way" in spite of her instructions.

Sam had warned her there would come a time when she'd have to put her foot down and make it clear who ran the show.

Claire crossed to the display, muscled the first chopper into the correct position, tilted the handlebars just so, then stepped back to admire the effect.

"You need help, ma'am?" Justin joined her.

"As a matter of fact, I do." She smiled patiently. "I left specific instructions for all the bikes in this display to have the front wheels point west. Why didn't that happen?"

Justin crossed his arms and tilted his head as he studied the bikes. "Well, I reminded Don of that this morning but he seemed to think Sam's old way was better."

"Last time I noticed, I was signing the checks around here now. So, which way do you think we should set these bikes?" Claire widened her eyes expectantly, sure Justin could deduce the correct answer.

The corner of his mouth twitched as he held back a grin. "I think they're gonna look real fine set up the way you want them."

She motioned with a crook of her finger for him to follow her across the room. She placed her back to the window. Justin mimicked her position, now standing where he could view the display as a customer would. The morning sunlight flashed on the spokes of the wheels like thousands of finely cut diamonds.

"There's more chrome on the carburetor side. That's what catches the customer's eye when they walk through the door, don't you think?" She watched for his reaction, wanting him to see the reason behind her request, but she'd have it her way whether he did or not.

He bobbed his head and gave her a two-fingered salute of understanding and approval.

"Consider it done," he confirmed.

"Thanks." She nodded, then continued down the narrow hallway to her office.

Claire dropped into the comfortable leather chair behind her desk for a quiet moment. Touching the ever-present cross at her throat, she reflected on the drama of her morning commute and the face she could not purge from her thoughts. Neither could she shake off the despair and terror of the innocent puppy.

Refusing to give in to the somber mood that threatened to settle over her heart, she swiveled to the credenza behind her desk and flipped the percolator's "on" switch, and began poring over Sam's computer programs. For the umpteenth time she marveled at the simplicity of what he had created when he'd turned his hobby into a thriving business.

"There's a visitor for you at the front counter," Justin's low Texas twang rumbled through the intercom speaker.

"I'm on my way."

She rolled the chair back as she stood, smoothed

her hands down the front of her crisp, linen slacks and tugged the hem of her jacket. Her heels clicked a staccato beat on the terra cotta tiles of the showroom floor as she crossed the room. She paused to refold a T-shirt and position it directly atop the stack, then straighten the hangers on a display rack.

Justin acknowledged her approach with a nod of his head and the man before the counter turned her way.

A polite smile curved his mouth and then the look of recognition she'd come to know spread to his eyes. The year of public display as Miss Texas and ensuing product endorsements would always be a business asset, even if the road to the title had been paved with her innocence.

"Claire Savage, I'd know you anywhere." His smile broadened. "It's great to finally meet you."

"The pleasure is all mine, sir." She accepted the stranger's outstretched hand. "Are you interested in a chopper? We're accepting deposits for the Southern Savage," she said, always promoting her dealership's soon-to-be-released signature bike.

"Actually, I'm interested in you." He released her from his grip to fish a business card from the coat pocket of his expensive designer suit. "The name's Arthur O'Malley—" he paused, seemingly for a reaction "—of *Today's Times* magazine." He emphasized the New York publication's name as he handed her the card.

Claire gave the response he obviously expected.

"*The* Arthur O'Malley? What an honor to have you pay my little store a visit."

His gaze swept the spacious area that warehoused several million dollars worth of dealer and aftermarket products, covering any biker's need.

He chuckled appreciation for her understatement.

"Could I interest you in dinner this evening to discuss how you came to be the proprietor of this *little store?*"

"Thanks for the invitation, but I have music rehearsal at my church tonight," she declined politely, having no intention of spending the evening deflecting the charm of a man old enough to be her father.

"And the name of that church would be...?" he probed like any good reporter should.

"My private business, if you don't mind." Claire refused his request. "What brings you to Houston?"

He got straight to the point. "I'm here doing some preliminary work for next month's international trade summit."

"At Savage Cycles we sell only American-made products, so I'm not certain we'd be of interest to you."

"Hmm, I was not aware of your policy, but it certainly lends a unique appeal to your philosophy of doing business, and might actually have more relevance than you know." He graced her with a practiced smile. "For my purposes anyway."

"Well, Mr. O'Malley, what *are* your purposes?"

"Please, call me Art," he requested, with a modest tilt of his head. "I'd like to interview you for an upcoming issue. Our 'Out of the Spotlight' editor is interested in doing a piece on the beauty queen turned motorcycle entrepreneur. You have to admit it's quite an unusual story."

Claire mentally flinched. That particular feature was usually reserved for has-been celebrities who'd dropped off the face of the earth after their fifteen minutes of fame. The final cut was often unflattering, turning up the heat on subjects to see what dirty secrets boiled to the surface.

Other than one piece of closely guarded information, there was no skeleton to rattle out of her closet. The name Claire Savage was synonymous with a squeaky clean reputation.

Still, the offer held appeal. Forced for most of her life to carefully manage every expense against her mother's small income, Claire's affinity for numbers kicked in to high gear. She considered the enormity of her professional debt.

Why not take advantage of the free publicity she could never afford otherwise?

"I can't deny the diversity of my accomplishments." She offered him the Mona Lisa smile and soft laugh that had charmed many a judge.

"Then you'll agree to the interview?" He seemed determined to close the deal.

"I'm afraid I'm not in a position to answer you today, but if you'll give me until Monday I'll consider it."

"Monday will be fine. I'm in town for a few days and then I'll be back next month for the summit. My private cell phone number is on the back of my card. You can reach me anytime, day or night."

She made a show of glancing at his number, then tucked the small card into her jacket pocket.

"And if you get hungry tonight after rehearsal…"

"I'll call you during business hours on Monday."

"I look forward to hearing from you, Claire."

He seemed to accept that their conversation had ended.

Through the showroom window she watched his rental car leave the lot and pull onto the interstate access road.

The advertised release date for her signature line was less than a month away. The timing of the *Today's Times* article couldn't be better. The prototype was complete and if all went according to plan, the release of the Southern Savage would secure her future in the custom design business. The opportunity seemed heaven-sent. How could she afford to pass?

Other than the canine rescue effort on the interstate that had delayed Luke Dawson's arrival at Abundant Harvest Church, the day was going according to plan. He drew a customized contract from his battered backpack and slid it across the low table that separated him from Pastor Ken Allen.

"Praise Productions will meet your expectations and those of your youth band or my services are free," Luke explained. "Our project will be considered complete when I've recorded your group, delivered your master CD and y'all are one hundred percent satisfied with the content and quality."

The senior pastor accepted the document and flipped slowly through the pages. As Ken made his initial scan of the contract, Luke studied the welcoming church leader, finding it easy to imagine why someone would pour his heart out to this charismatic man.

An act Luke was not tempted in the least to do.

"The conditions I mentioned are all spelled out in the agreement. My work history is attached, and I'm happy to answer any questions." He paused again to give the pastor time to read.

Luke had spent the past hour pitching the services of Praise Productions, his mobile one-man recording company. His offer of a free two-day rehearsal and subsequent audition normally sealed the deal. As a rule, once the pastor and his council checked Luke's references and observed his work, they were anxious to secure his services. Luke prayed the usual process would work once again, and that he wouldn't have to reveal his personal reasons for coming to Abundant Harvest.

"I don't accept deposits or ask for any portion of my fee up front," he explained. "Full payment will only be expected after you approve of the master. If you have a valid complaint within the first year, I guarantee a full refund. I'm proud to say that's never been necessary."

The pastor glanced up and Luke continued.

"There's a list of duplication houses attached to the contract. I try to include some local referrals, but sometimes you have to go out of state to get the best deal. I always leave that choice up to the decision makers at the church."

Pastor Allen narrowed his eyes as he fixed Luke with an assessing stare. "I've read about production companies in Nashville and Los Angeles. Seems to me, staying in one spot would be simpler for a growing enterprise." He paused to level Luke with a curious gaze. "Why do you spend your life on the road, son?"

Luke smiled and relaxed in his chair.

"I love the industry, but it's competitive and cutthroat. I don't care to live in any of the U.S. production meccas and I don't want a big company choosing my projects for me. So, I opted to be portable and stay independent. I research and select my own clients, manage the process from start to finish, and when the work is done I move on to new challenges in a new part of the country."

The trim pastor reached into a large candy dish

in the middle of the table and withdrew a bite-size chocolate bar. He offered one to Luke and took two for himself.

"Luke, it's not my place to question your financial practices, but I've already put some research into recording costs and your rates are significantly lower than any I've seen. I'd almost feel guilty, like we were taking advantage of you."

"Sir, I assure you there's no need to feel that way. Earning a fortune at this isn't my goal and I have resources that allow me to be flexible."

Luke referred to his dependency upon the dwindling earnings of the heavy metal band he put together during his boarding school days. As the infamous and outrageous Striker Dark, Luke was the front man on lead guitar and vocals. His out-of-control life as Striker drove the final wedge between Luke and his rigidly conservative parents, who wouldn't forgive their son's choices, even today.

In the early years a staggering amount of money had allowed him to make a clean break from his folks and never look back. Before signing with an unscrupulous agent he'd lived like a prince, but Lisa Evans had managed the band out of a fortune that should have lasted a lifetime. The loss of Luke's income to a money-hungry woman was now at the top of a long list of mistakes he never intended to make again.

Fortunately, all these years later a new generation of rockers found the old albums. The royalties steadily trickled in for the band that had held the attention of the American public and the music industry for six years.

Until tragedy split them up.

"I'm sorry. I didn't mean to pry into your private business," the pastor's voice interrupted Luke's thoughts.

"No apology necessary, sir." Luke unwrapped his candy and popped the sweet confection into his mouth.

"Then that leaves the question of why us? You said you were in California the past year. How did you hear about Abundant Harvest Church?"

"Like I said, I do my research. I've been exposed on one level or another to the recording industry since I was a kid. I've seen a lot of talent destroyed by the trappings of the business and I believe God's called me to help young people avoid some of the dangers. I watched this year's Battle of the Bands review online and came to see if the Harvest Sons are as promising as they seem."

Absolutely true, but not the whole story.

The real draw was the young man who played lead guitar for the Harvest Sons. A ringer for Luke at that age, obviously filled with startling promise and easy prey for a gold-digging agent. The boy's image had haunted Luke, who was impressed to the point of distraction during the hours he'd studied the video. He'd been drawn to Houston by a force too big to fight. He was on a mission to satisfy himself that the kid named Eric would not suffer the same fate as Striker Dark.

Pastor Ken looked at his watch, stood and motioned for Luke to follow. "The band uses the main sanctuary to practice before the evening service. Let's go see if the Sons live up to their reputation."

"Sir—" Luke paused before standing "—I should warn you about my no-nonsense style. I don't mince words and I've been known to step on more than a few toes. But it works for me and I'll pit my results against anybody's any day."

Ken smiled, grabbed another bite of candy and tossed one to Luke. "As I recall, Jesus was a pretty direct communicator."

"Yeah, and look how popular He was with the Pharisees," Luke quipped, and the two men chuckled as they passed through the doorway.

Saturday afternoons were always a time of bustling activity at Abundant Harvest. Claire made a habit of being on-site each week whether or not she'd signed up for volunteer work. By all standards this church had a large congregation with a perpetual need for unscheduled help. Arriving early, she parked at the outer edge of the lot, collected her purse and book bag and began the hike toward the main sanctuary.

She stopped short at the sight of an unmarked black truck and matching gooseneck trailer that stretched across a half-dozen parking spaces. The combo would be commonplace at Savage cycles, however, in the church parking lot it was an unexpected and imposing sight.

Shrieks of obvious delight and the excited yapping of a dog drew her thoughts from the black rig. Claire changed her course and followed the sounds to the temporary classrooms positioned behind the youth center known as the Hangar.

"Hi, Miss Claire!" a gaggle of girls called. Three high school seniors perched with legs swinging on the tailgate of a friend's muddy pickup. Their attention was immediately diverted by barking and laughter.

"What's all the fuss?"

"The guys are teaching this puppy to play Frisbee," one of them explained. "He's a natural but he doesn't want to give it back after he catches it. Brian and Eric will be too tired to play for the service tonight if they keep this up."

Peals of laughter rose from the growing crowd of high schoolers. Claire navigated the parking lot to the edge of the grass, where lively activity was in full swing. At the sight of a yellow Lab pup, a stab of anguish shot through her heart as she remembered the scene only hours earlier. But this well-groomed dog sported a red bandana around his neck, brandished a white Frisbee in his mouth and proudly ran the boys a merry chase.

Brian dived for the animal's skinny hind legs and missed by a long shot. The dog whirled about, trotted back to where Brian lay facedown in the grass, dropped the Frisbee on the boy's head and woofed in chorus with the kids' laughter.

Claire took in the relaxed scene, wondering if these youngsters had any idea how fortunate they were to be so carefree. At their age she'd had precious little time for weekend afternoons of games and laughter. There were voice lessons and costume fittings, rehearsals and rounds of competition.

Even in the quiet of her room at night she never forgot that one small mistake could cost her everything. After her father left to chase his dreams, the life she and her mother salvaged depended upon vigilance and dedication. To secure her tuition at the acclaimed private school she had to have scholarships. She had to win pageants.

She had to look and sound perfect.

Light glinted through the trees as the sun dipped toward the western skyline, reminding her the afternoon was winding down. Her chance to practice in the sanctuary was slipping away. Tomorrow morning's solo would challenge her vocal range and she wanted one final sound check, so she headed toward the main auditorium.

By design, every aspect of Abundant Harvest Church was contemporary. Shunning the traditional redbrick chapel with a long center aisle, the church founders had opted to invest their building funds in an economical and practical 70,000 square foot warehouse-style structure.

The facility known as the worship center served as a sanctuary for weekend services. When the hundreds of folding chairs were stored away, the expansive room became a double-sized gymnasium for after-school activities. Each week visitors made notes on their welcome cards expressing approval of the spacious accommodations, including a stage with state-of-the-art audio/visual equipment.

Familiar with the Saturday evening sound crew, Claire waved to the figures, barely visible through the darkened window of the control booth, and climbed six steps that led up the right side of the stage.

"Good afternoon, Claire," the pastor's voice boomed from the speakers.

She raised her hand, palm outward, against the glare of lights being set for the evening service.

"Hi, Pastor Ken." She waved a response into the darkness.

The band's self-appointed stage manager, Dana Stabler, positioned a microphone before Claire. The petite brunette was a quirky teen who tried on personalities like other girls experimented with nail color. Today she was hip-hop, all decked out in baggy jeans and a football jersey.

"Ready?" she asked.

"Give me a minute, Dana." Claire turned her back to the mic. After practicing some warm-up scales, she dropped her chin and offered up a silent prayer. Then she turned toward the light and removed the microphone from its stand.

She inhaled through her nose and opened her mouth to begin. Before the first note rushed across her vocal chords, a voice intruded.

"One moment, miss." A polite command, not a suggestion.

With her mouth gaping open in surprise she felt and probably looked like a hungry guppy. Her lips clamped together with a small "umph" as she waited for some cue to continue.

"Go ahead, please," the voice instructed.

Claire closed her eyes to concentrate and recall the note to be sung a cappella, without accompaniment. Once again she filled her lungs, parted her lips and began to breathe the high C. The note started softly, low in her chest, then crescendoed over the course of several seconds into a force of sound that filled her head and resonated in the open hall.

She'd tilted her head back from the mic allowing the sound to float heavenward. A high-pitched squeal pierced the moment. Her head and eyes snapped toward the source of the disturbance.

"Sorry about that," was the curt response from the booth.

"Is there a problem?" Claire asked, knowing her

voice held a hint of the annoyance she was feeling after the back-to-back interruptions.

"There's a new guy in the sound booth." Dana's pierced eyebrows drew together apologetically.

"I noticed." Claire curved her lips into a wry smile.

"Take it from the top," the male voice suggested.

"If you're sure." She squinted against the lights.

"I'm sure." There was amusement in his otherwise brusque tone. "I'm also sure less vibrato will make your intro more powerful."

"Excuse me?" No one had criticized her skills since she'd fired her last vocal coach.

"Control the vibrato, *if you can*," the man challenged.

Five seconds into the opening note the voice once again interrupted, "Cutting that high C off sooner will give you more breath for the next measure. Would you like to practice off mic before we begin again?"

Claire jammed a fist on each hip as she glared into the darkness. The huge room fell silent awaiting her response.

"Are you just gonna stand there in a double huff?" he asked.

She was positive she heard the guy snicker.

"Pastor Ken, may I speak with you for a moment?" Claire planted the mic back into the stand and headed down the steps. She took several unsure paces up the aisle, as she waited for her pupils to make the switch from white-hot spotlights to the dimly lit auditorium.

A side door opened, allowing slanting rays of afternoon sun to pour inside. She was distracted from her mission as all heads turned to follow the progress of a runaway pup, barking with obvious pleasure and loping up the aisle toward Claire with a half-dozen teens in hot pursuit.

Chapter Two

Her agitation forgotten, Claire gave in to the force of a smile as it spread across her face at the unusual sight. This particular animal was so energized and jubilant that, for a few seconds anyway, nobody seemed anxious to curtail the pup's activity.

On stage, where Dana continued to set up the band for the evening service, she crossed one mic path over another and a screech of feedback blared.

The dog darted beneath a row of seats, crouched in the darkness and whined in puppy terror.

A male figure left the sound booth, navigating the darkened aisle in long, determined strides.

"My apologies, folks. I'll take care of this."

The voice was soft and humble, but definitely the same one that recently questioned her skills.

"Hang on, Freeway. I've got you, buddy." He held

up a hand to ward off the approaching teens, a quiet signal the situation was under control.

Dropping to one knee, he extended his arm, palm to the floor and allowed the dog to sniff cautiously. The sniffing soon turned to contented licking and happy tail thumping. The puppy crept from beneath the seat and into the waiting arms of a master who cradled the pet in a gentle embrace. "Freeway trusts me," he said simply.

Claire's breath caught in her throat at the overwhelming sense of familiarity.

"Sorry about that, Pastor Ken," Brian apologized for the group, then herded everyone toward the door.

"No harm done," the pastor assured them. "Give us fifteen and we'll be ready for you guys."

"I'll put Freeway on a lead and find him a shady spot for a nap."

"Great idea, Luke. That'll give Claire time to finish her sound check."

Claire was positioned in the aisle between the open door and the stranger in the shadows. She stepped aside to allow him to pass. Each step brought him closer to her.

Closer to the light.

"Oh, forgive my lack of manners." Pastor Ken hurried to Claire's side. "Hit the house lights, please," he called to a volunteer and the florescent bulbs overhead blazed to life.

"Claire Savage, I'd like to introduce Luke Dawson. Luke, Claire is the young woman with the incredible voice I was telling you about."

She reached to steady herself on the back of a nearby folding chair. Standing before her was the Good Samaritan who had monopolized her thoughts for the better part of the day.

Luke clenched his teeth and waited for the response that almost always accompanied an introduction. People never said anything out loud, not in front of him anyway. But unspoken pity for his permanent disfigurement was there. Loud and clear.

If they only knew he'd been through fourteen grueling procedures to get to this point. Skin grafts were amazing, not magical, and there was a limit to what reconstructive surgery could accomplish. The remaining scar on his neck was the last remnant of the fire and a constant reminder of the all-consuming demon that was only a snort away. He'd long ago accepted the ugly scar on his neck. And in an oddly comforting way, facing the vestige of his freebasing accident in the mirror every day kept him from slipping back into the pit of his destructive past.

He shifted Freeway's lanky frame and extended a hand. She hesitated before dropping her purse onto the seat of the nearest chair and accepting his grasp.

"Pleased to meet you," she said, and for once a greeting surprised him.

Sincere interest flickered through the molasses-brown eyes fringed with thick lashes. It usually took a few minutes of polite conversation and the mention of his profession to solicit that wide-eyed, raised-eyebrow look. Was she going to run right past sympathy and slide into open and outright curiosity? This was a first.

Most folks seemed eager to keep the contact brief, as if the disfigurement on his neck was transmissible. This woman held on, prolonging the grip, all the while her eyes fixed on his. She appeared to size him up through the touch. He had to admit it was an appealing change, and the closest thing to intimate contact he'd allowed in years.

Her blunt cut hair had glistened under the stage lights with too many shades of blond to be anything but natural. It hung straight, just past her shoulders, with bangs that could use a trim. She was tall. The kind of tall that had probably cost her a date to the prom because high school boys were too cowardly to dance with her. Shoulders back, chin high, she looked him eyeball to eyeball with no apology for her height.

Something about the almost overconfident gleam in her dark eyes caused him a moment of discomfort. Of déjà vu.

He shifted his attention to her dress. She'd opted for trousers and a jacket on a day of record Houston heat. He was certainly in no position to judge since he stood there in his perpetual "uniform," consisting of jeans and a long sleeved black T-shirt with *Praise Productions* printed in script across the back.

"Claire Savage," he slowly repeated her name as he released her hand.

She trailed her fingers lightly over Freeway's head and paused at his long nose allowing the pup to take in her scent and taste. The sure sign of an animal lover.

"If her name rings a bell it's because a few years back Claire was Miss Texas and first runner-up for Miss America. She did a bunch of those milk commercials." Pastor Ken offered the information over one shoulder as he returned to his evening duties.

"No, I couldn't possibly know you from that. I've never been subjected to a beauty pageant and hopefully never will. Sorry." Luke shook his head.

"Understandable." She chuckled. "Woman parading before judges in beaded evening gowns is not everybody's cup of tea." Then, her gaze narrowed slightly, the brown of her eyes deepened as she appeared to study him. "And no need to apologize, Luke…" She hesitated.

"Dawson," he reminded her.

"Dawson," she drew his name out slowly. She impaled him with a stare that spoke louder than words and the déjà vu made sense. Lisa Evans. The way this beauty sized him up with her eyes reminded him of the first time he'd met Lisa.

"My fifteen minutes of fame were fairly regional," Claire continued, "so it's not like I was ever a famous celebrity or a notorious rock star."

The threat of trouble bubbled up from his core. He'd built an honorable profession by keeping a low profile. Facial reconstruction had disguised him so thoroughly that retreat had never been necessary. But as the saying went, there was a first time for everything. So he followed his gut and changed the subject.

"The only thing notorious around here will be Freeway if I don't get him off this floor and out to the grass."

"Oh, sure," she agreed. She gave the yellow paw a light squeeze and stepped out of their path.

Claire admired what seemed to be an amazing lack of self-consciousness on his part. The damage to his neck was an obvious sign that he'd been the victim of a fire.

Growing up in a world where every physical imperfection had to be identified, analyzed and corrected, she had a vivid idea of how he must have suffered inside. But there was no sign of residual pain as he left the auditorium and the heavy door closed softly at his back.

"Miss Claire, the mics are all set now. You want to give it one more try?" Dana called.

"Of course. Maybe with our new critic outside I'll be able to get past my first note." She poked fun at the earlier annoyance as she climbed the steps to the stage and resumed her effort to perfect her number.

* * *

As they rehearsed, Luke assessed the boys who called themselves the Harvest Sons, his eyes trained like lasers on the kid in front. At first glance the four were just a promising cover band, but on closer observation Luke noted ability that went beyond mere talent. These kids were gifted musicians, but they needed professional help.

Houston's Battle of the Bands festival had gained national attention when the winning group appeared on a network entertainment show. Luke did some homework and found out the Spring Break event offered kids in a dozen states a safe alternative to the temptations of Mexican beaches. The largest high school music competition in the Southwest had become a phenomenon, attracting the attention of music producers and record label executives. The March festival had ended with the Harvest Sons in third place, an incredible showing for a Christian group.

During their meeting Ken had mentioned the boys' disappointment at their number-three status, and their request for assistance from the church council to cover professional training. So, nobody appeared particularly surprised by the pastor's statement that night.

"I'm pleased to announce that Mr. Luke Dawson, the owner of Praise Productions, has offered to spend the next two days auditioning with us. Luke's professional services include coaching, developing and recording youth praise bands. If we can reach a mutual agreement, he's going to work with our boys to record a CD."

Beaming their approval, the boys high-fived as the small crowd erupted into applause. Pastor Ken motioned for Luke to join him on the stage. Claire turned along with the others to look in Luke's direction. He remained in his relaxed position, right shoulder leaning against the wall, not more than ten feet from where she sat. He lifted a hand to wave a brief greeting but shook his head to indicate his refusal to leave his post.

"Well, I see our guest is going to be reluctant to share the spotlight with this talented group of young men." The pastor turned toward the musicians. "But don't let that modest response fool you, guys. Luke has given his word that he'll whip you into tip-top shape or his services are free."

The adults in the room mouthed collective disbelief and glanced at one another for confirmation of such a commitment. Turn the four high school kids into professionals in a couple of weeks or work for nothing? Quite a gesture from a total stranger.

Claire began her habit of mentally calculating the cost of such an offer. Could this man's generosity be covering some fine print that could put the church at risk? As head of the finance committee she'd make sure the church was not left holding some financial bag if this guy fell short on his end of the deal. She squinted for a better look at his face, for a clue to his intentions.

He stood with feet planted wide, solid arms folded across his chest, staring forward at some invisible point without making eye contact. While a smile played at his mouth, and his eyes crinkled in conjunction, no spark of joy lit his gaze. He only smiled for the sake of the observers. After all the years of painting that same expression on her face to guard the feelings inside, she recognized the ambivalent stare of a kindred spirit.

A person with something to hide.

She brushed bangs out of her eyes and swept her hand across the gold cross at her throat. *If* the man had secrets, he was certainly entitled to them, just as she was. As long as they stayed buried too deeply to cause harm to these impressionable boys, who was she to judge? Still, she would be cautious.

Claire would make sure any agreement between Praise Productions and Abundant Harvest was legal and fail-safe for the church that was her family.

Luke worshipped with the congregation that evening from the privacy of the audio/visual booth. During the musical numbers, he observed the equipment and the young female volunteer whose hands moved capably across the dials and levers of the soundboard. The mixing capacity of the Praise

Productions mobile unit would more than compensate for any lack of local technology.

He'd gritted his teeth several times during the band's amateurish performance, but silently applauded the contribution of each member. Shaggy-haired Zach paid too much attention to the girls in the front row. Even so, his drumming was impressive. You could tell he was holding back, itching to liven up the arrangements and break into a rock beat. Given the right musical vehicle he would wow a crowd.

Chad was a prodigy at the keyboard. Luke was certain from the boy's rigid stance that the teen had been classically trained. With encouragement to loosen up, the bespectacled youth would give any piano man a run for his money.

Brian appeared to be the youngest in the group. Sullen and quiet, his bass was rumbling and low, soulful to the untrained observer. To Luke's ear it was downright painful. The instrument begged to be tuned to pitch. But the boy had great hands and a keen sense of rhythm. He could be groomed.

Then there was Eric, clearly the leader of the band, and Brian's older brother. Luke swallowed to ease the tightness in his throat as he watched the boy that the others looked to as their spokesman. Eric lovingly cradled the custom figured Gibson Les Paul guitar like a treasured friend. The long fingers of his left hand wrapped the neck of the instrument while his right hand plucked a sweet melody from the six strings.

Eric closed his eyes, communed with the instrument and seemed to feel the sound to his core. Luke's heart ached for the enchanted pair as he recognized long buried parts of himself in the boy and the guitar.

A sense of purpose he'd never felt before stole over Luke. As if the Holy Spirit whispered in Luke's ear, he knew an unusual moment of being at peace.

He'd made the right decision to seek out this kid. He could make a difference here.

The service ended and worshipers streamed from the building as the evening crowd went home to their Saturday night routines. With lights blazing inside the sanctuary, Luke made his way down to the front of the nearly empty auditorium.

Eric looked up from the business of snapping the lid on his guitar case.

"What did you think, Mr. Dawson?"

"Call me Luke, but don't be so quick to pack up. We have serious work to do." He glanced around at the others. "Any of you guys working tomorrow or playing for the early service?"

"No, sir," they chorused.

"Good." He held a set of church keys aloft and rattled them for emphasis. "We have a lot of ground to cover before we audition on Monday evening and Pastor Ken says we're free to practice anytime the sanctuary is not reserved. I'm a natural night owl. Think you guys can keep up with me?"

Four pairs of eyes flew wide. The suggestion that they hang around well after normal hours was obviously a novel one. They looked to Eric for a response.

"Sure!" His head wagged agreeably.

"Then y'all call your folks and get permission to stay late."

Luke would find out fast whether or not they were serious about their craft. If the band was willing to work, and work hard, he could take them to the next level and higher in a couple of intense weeks. When he handed over a master recording there would be no doubt in anyone's mind that Praise Productions had fulfilled the agreement.

Claire couldn't believe her ears. She'd already hung around hours longer than necessary just to keep an eye on things. She was singing at the early service and needed to go home to feed the animals, review a stack of spreadsheets and get a good night's rest.

She hurried to the main entrance and pushed the door wide in time to see the taillights of the pastor's black pickup fade into the trees. He obviously trusted this guy to give him total access to the building. The door fell closed with a thud and five heads turned in her direction.

They were a team. She was an intruder.

"You're still here." Luke's voice was flat, grouchy. He was not pleased.

"Yes." She searched for a reason to justify her presence. "I overheard you asking the guys to hang around and thought I might stay and offer my help. As Pastor Ken mentioned, I've had quite a bit of musical training myself."

Luke's expression softened. He actually smiled.

A charming smile. A lazy smile that ignited a spark of mischief in his eyes and caused her to pull in a deep breath to cover the odd beating of her heart.

"Matter of fact, I would appreciate your help."

As he walked toward her he reached into his back pocket and pulled out a faded brown wallet. He plucked a twenty-dollar bill from the folded leather and held it toward her.

"I saw a taco stand up the road. How about getting us all a hot meal and giving Freeway a quick walk around the parking lot? I can send one of the boys with you if you're afraid to go alone," he challenged.

If being the gofer gave her a reason to stick around, so be it.

"Sure, I'll be glad to do that. But when I get back I thought we might be able to collaborate."

"Collaborate?" One dark eyebrow arched skeptically.

"You know, offer one another assistance based on our musical backgrounds."

He cracked that lazy grin again and there was no denying it. Her heart definitely thumped double time.

"I'm glad you brought up the subject of assistance, because you could use some work on that piece you were rehearsing. That arrangement is all wrong for your voice but I can give you some suggestions to get you through it if you want to stick around a while longer."

She snatched the twenty from his fingers and stuffed it into her purse.

"Thanks, I'll think about it," she muttered as she spun about-face and stomped up the aisle. She heard the rumble of his laughter just before she pushed through the security door into the muggy night air.

A Harvard MBA sent to fetch burritos. Miss Texas being asked to walk the dog. A guy she didn't know from Adam criticizing her musical arrangement. If she weren't so tired she'd indulge in a self-righteous hissy fit. She settled instead for slamming the door of her coupe a little harder than necessary.

As the pony car approached the late night drive-thru, the mature businesswoman in her toyed with a teenage prank. Claire's huffy mood evaporated and a grin crept across her face. If the newcomer was going to treat her like one of the kids he'd better be prepared to suffer the consequences.

Chapter Three

"And put extra jalapeños on those two super tacos, please." Claire smirked at the giant piñata head that returned her grin blindly and bobbed its approval of her diabolical plan.

"I have to warn you, ma'am. The super taco already comes with enough peppers to heat Minnesota in January," the night manager of the restaurant replied.

"I know, but I'm just relaying the order. The man specifically said he wanted his meal 'hot.'"

"Okaa-aa-aay, but he's gonna be miserable tomorrow."

"That's the plan," she muttered under her breath as she eased the car forward to the carry-out window.

With a sack of fragrant Tex-Mex on the bucket seat beside her and the warm evening breeze whipping through the open windows, Claire made the short drive back to the church. Determined to see this guy's true colors, she crept inside the sanctuary to a seat in the shadows. The less she disturbed the more she could observe. If anyone noticed her arrival they didn't acknowledge it.

Luke was taking the group through one of the numbers they'd played for the evening service, stopping them frequently as he'd done Claire during her practice run. Like a professional coach who insists a championship team start every drill with the basics, Luke singled out each boy and went over the fundamentals of his instrument. Though they reviewed familiar territory, the newcomer seemed to give each student a fresh sense of timing or tuning or the history of the instrument before moving on.

A series of high-pitched beeps emanated from Eric's backpack. He cradled his guitar in the upright stand and reached for his cell phone.

"Unless that's your mother, don't answer it," Luke commanded.

"Nobody calls him *but* his mother," Zach sniped and the others snickered.

Eric gave a sidelong glance at the caller ID and punched the ignore button. Luke held his hand out and the cell phone was deposited into his open palm.

"Any others?" Luke's tone left no doubt about what was expected.

Pockets were emptied and four flip phones ended

up single file on top of an amplifier. Her Blackberry was set on vibrate but, unwilling to risk being discovered, Claire reached into her purse and silently depressed the "off" key.

"This is as good a time as any to spell out expectations." Luke lowered his lean frame to the stage floor, folded long legs beneath him and motioned for the guys to do the same. They sat cross-legged in a circle like silent scouts around a campfire.

"Well? Speak up," Luke snapped, then waited for a response. The boys cast one another unsure glances.

"Shouldn't you tell us *your* expectations, sir," Zach asked, as he nervously rolled a drumstick between his palms.

Luke shook his head. "Let's get this straight. This isn't about me or Praise Productions. It's about the Harvest Sons. If you don't know what you want, how can we move you to the next level?" Luke waited through several seconds of silence. "Talk to me," he insisted. "Just share what's on your minds."

"The sound is pretty good in here," Zach said, glancing at the high ceiling, "but I have to hold back. My dream is to rock an outdoor stadium before I'm in my thirties like you and too old to enjoy it."

Teenage heads nodded agreement and Luke grimaced, "Gee, thanks."

"You know what I mean." Zach studied his drumstick, clearly chagrined by his tactless admission.

"Yes, I'm afraid I do," Luke grumbled, but winked at the others to let Zach see no offense was taken.

Chad spoke up. "Since I was seven I've been at the keyboard ten hours a week, twenty in the summer. I can mimic any style, but I wanna be known for a sound of my own. I want the Sons to play more than cover tunes and jazzed up hymns."

"Now we're getting somewhere." Luke nodded at Chad, then turned. "How about you, Eric?"

"The only good thing our dad ever did was name me after Eric Clapton. He's a triple inductee into the Rock and Roll Hall of Fame." Eric's eyes lit as he warmed to the subject of his rock hero. "I learned most of what I know by playing along with his CDs. I'd love to have a reputation like Clapton's one day," Eric admitted. "But only on the guitar," he quickly added. "I'd never be stupid like he was with coke and heroin. Musicians who blow their careers over drugs are so lame."

Luke brushed his palm across his short-cropped hair, before dropping his hand back into his lap.

"You'd be surprised how easy it is to fall into that trap, Eric."

Claire caught the slightly defensive note in his voice.

"Are you saying what he did was okay?" Chad asked.

"Absolutely not," Luke insisted. "But you should have some compassion for what drove Clapton down the road he chose."

"Nobody deserves compassion for making such stupid choices," Eric insisted. "His drug abuse will label him for the rest of his life."

There was an uncomfortable silence for a few moments as Luke seemed to think about the judgmental comment.

"Good point, Eric. All a man really has to call his own is his reputation, and once that's damaged it's just about impossible to make repairs."

Then he moved on. "And what do you want from this experience, Brian?"

The young bass player slumped, exhaled a pent-up breath and fiddled with the plastic guitar pick between his fingers.

"Brian wants to make it in the business so he can get away from our old man," Eric offered on behalf of his kid brother.

"Forever," Brian added, not looking up.

Claire noted the way Luke's gaze darted back and forth between the two brothers, taking in that piece of news. She squirmed in her dark corner of the room, uncomfortable, feeling she was eavesdropping on group therapy. Luke was making a sincere, albeit gruff effort to get to know his protégés. Even grudgingly, she had to admire that in the man.

"Believe it or not, guys, I understand. At your age I felt all those things. Thanks for being honest with me." Luke's voice was hushed, almost reverent. She had to lean forward and listen closely.

"Now that I know why you're here we can start plotting some serious progress. If you knuckle down and really work hard for me, what we accomplish in the next two days will blow your minds. But I warn you, I can't abide slackers. I have to prove myself to your church council, and you guys have to prove yourselves to me. Got that?"

Heads bobbed agreement as he glanced around the circle.

"I never make a promise I can't keep. So, listen up. When you work with me you'll stretch your skills and your minds and I promise we'll produce music that will open doors for you in this business. But when we're working together you've got to give me your undivided attention, and I'll do the same for you. No exceptions. You got that, too?"

They nodded understanding.

Luke extended his arm into the center of the circle, palm down and asked, "Are we a team?"

Hands stacked on hands as they shared that very male ritual of the pregame huddle followed by high fives.

"Hey, Miss Texas, you got anything to eat back there?"

When Luke called out his question young heads turned her way. Startled to realize he'd known she was there all along, Claire jumped to her feet, grabbed the bag of fast food and hurried down front.

"Thanks, Miss Claire!"

The youngsters took the bag, fished out burritos and napkins and tossed the sack and remaining contents to Luke. He pulled several bills from his wallet and sent them to the soft drink machines in the basement kitchen with stern instructions to hurry back.

"Still sore at me?" His brows arched expectantly over green eyes, his mouth quirked with a hint of humor.

"Why would you ask that?" She played the wide-eyed dumb blonde, and hated herself for it.

"Oh, maybe because I yanked your chain a few times, but just to see if you were a good sport."

"And?" She waited, for some strange reason hoping she'd overcome the prima donna, first impression she may have given him.

"And you reacted like a professional."

She could tell he wanted to say more.

"But?" She stuffed her hands in her jacket pockets and waited for the rest.

"But even pros make mistakes. That's a popular piece of music that everybody will recognize, but it's all wrong for your voice. If you wanna give your best performance you'll let me coach you." He threw down the gauntlet, something he appeared to do frequently.

"Oh, that's not necessary." She brushed off his suggestion.

"Trust me. It is."

"Speaking of trust," she changed the subject, "I understand why Freeway trusts you. I was there this morning when you rescued him on the bridge. That was a brave thing you did."

"Bravery had nothin' to do with it." He brushed away the compliment like a pesky fly. "I just couldn't help myself. It makes me so mad to see an animal or a kid mistreated."

Squeaking sneakers and the muffled voices of four teens signaled they were about to have company. Luke looked down and focused on the meal. He rustled inside the white paper sack and withdrew a taco. He peeled back the wrapper and prepared to take a large bite.

"Wait!" Claire shouted, regretting her juvenile act, making a sudden effort to stop him. But he leaned out of her reach and sunk his teeth into the crisp corn tortilla, loaded with three-alarm salsa and jalapeño peppers.

Luke scrunched his forehead in a scowl as he dodged the woman's attempt to grab his taco. The salty shell broke in his mouth with a crunch. Tasty meat seasoned with hot sauce filled his senses. As he chewed he became aware of the spicy warmth that quickly morphed into a burning sensation. Within seconds his breath caught in his throat. His mouth and sinuses blazed.

Claire sprinted toward the door where Zach had appeared, an unopened soda in his hand. She scooped it from his grip and tossed it in a high arch directly at Luke. In a fluid movement he caught the can, popped the top, dodged the spray and chugged the soda. He stopped to draw a breath only to ensure his esophagus hadn't suffered permanent damage.

"I'm so sorry!" Claire stood at his side, her hands clenched together at her heart as if pleading for forgiveness.

Luke continued to let the chilly effervescence of the drink soothe the coals that still smoldered inside his mouth.

Pure mortification in her eyes, Claire held out her hand for the remainder of his meal. Instead Luke plopped the empty can in her palm and took a close look at the offending taco. It was packed with hot peppers, each seed a tiny grenade of heat waiting to explode. He crammed it back into the sack, unwrapped, and examined a second taco that was also crowded with ripe green jalapeños. He turned to the woman who'd literally taken his breath away.

"How thoughtful of you to welcome a newcomer to your church with a meal that's obviously a special order." He spoke loud enough for the boys to hear and they naturally drifted toward the couple to find out what effort Claire had gone to for their new mentor.

Her eyes widened as Luke extended his hand, waving the peppery fare beneath her nose. "Care to share with me?"

"No, thanks." She shook her head, an adamant refusal that brushed a cascade of fine blond hair across her shoulders. "I never eat this late at night."

"Oh, come on now. How much can one bite hurt?" Luke cajoled, knowing full well how painful one bite would be.

"Yeah, Miss Claire, you're too skinny," Zach chimed in. "Eat up."

The group of boys surrounded her, insisting she share the food Luke continued to offer. She waved Luke away but he caught her wrist, rotated her hand and deposited the taco into her palm. He lifted his eyebrows expectantly, a silent dare only she would understand.

Trepidation written all over her unforgettable face, she licked her lips as if anticipating the fire. The paper wrapper rustled as she squeezed the taco and brought it closer to her face. She eyed the heap of peppers, swallowed what must have been her pride and closed her eyes as if blocking the thought of the approaching inferno.

Luke enjoyed the way her perfect little nose twitched when it caught the vinegary scent of the peppers. He was sure she'd back down, but she resolutely parted her lips and prepared to take the plunge.

He was impressed.

He clapped his hands together loudly to capture everyone's attention. Claire's eyes flew wide at the noisy interruption. Her mouth clamped shut narrowly avoiding the peppery snack only moments from her lips.

"Okay, everybody, let's get busy." Luke waved them toward the stage.

When the boys had turned their backs she exhaled her relief, dropped the hazardous taco into the open sack and mouthed "I'm sorry." The sincerity of the silent apology showed in her caramel-brown eyes but the small smirk that wriggled at the corners of her mouth said otherwise. She ducked her head too late to hide the smile.

"I'll just clean up back here and be on my way." Claire bent to gather her belongings.

"Not so fast," he snapped.

Her head popped up at the insistent tone in his voice.

He masked his thoughts with a blank face and inclined his head in the direction the boys were heading.

"It's time for me to repay your *kindness*." He stressed the last word, a warning of what was to come.

Her eyebrows rose in question.

"Chad, go to the booth and cue the lady's music," Luke called out.

She glanced at her wristwatch, any excuse to break contact with those demanding green eyes. "It's getting late and you have other commitments."

"And miss the opportunity to *collaborate?* Not on your life." Refusing to take "no" for an answer, he stepped aside and motioned for her to precede him up the aisle.

Two hours later, Claire sat before the computer in her southwest Houston townhome. Surrounded by her menagerie of foster pets, she arched her back and yawned as she waited for the final search engine to work its powerful magic.

Buck squirmed and buried his nose beneath her arm. She'd long since mastered the art of typing with the abused dachshund in her lap. R.C. perched nearby, dangling his long tail over the arm of Claire's favorite chair. The red tabby cat would find himself relegated to the garage if he sharpened his claws on the leather recliner again.

Aptly named for his three-legged status, Tripod dozed on the rug beside her, his sides rising and falling in conjunction with his noisy breathing. The Airedale's costly asthma was the primary reason he was still without a permanent home.

With one hand Claire snuggled Buck closer and with the other she reached to trail her fingers across Tripod's wiry head. He opened adoring eyes, sighed his gratitude and drifted back into doggie dreamland. She understood the contentment these abandoned animals felt in the sanctuary of her home.

Two weeks after Claire's thirteenth birthday, Dean

Savage dealt his family a staggering blow. He was moving to L.A. to pursue his dream of being an actor. Alone.

To Claire's astonishment Mary Savage didn't plead with her husband to stay. Instead she sought comfort in her Bible as Claire's father packed, muttering under his breath about women and their religious nonsense. The next day he was gone, leaving Claire and her mother with nothing more than the roof over their heads.

The computer beeped to signal its work was complete.

She scanned the results of her search on Praise Productions, disappointed to find no home page, odd for a growing business. There were numerous brief blurbs in relation to churches Praise Productions had worked with in the recent past. All glowing reports, nothing of concern. She should be relieved instead of feeling like she'd come up empty-handed, just as she had for the search under Luke's name, yielding only pages of genealogy listings.

She looped the gold chain around her index finger and cupped the diamond cross in her hand. The grudging respect and strange attraction she felt for the man with the lazy smile conflicted with her need to protect her Abundant Harvest family.

The guy had some unique qualities but he was running stealth for a reason. Tomorrow Claire would go over his contract with a fine-tooth comb. She might even call her Texas Ranger friend, Daniel Stabler, for a background check. If Luke Dawson was hiding something, she'd pull the plug on the deal faster than you could say Savage Cycles of Houston.

Chapter Four

Sunday morning Luke twisted the knob and the door of his furnished efficiency swung open.

Home sweet home.

He surveyed his surroundings, nodding approval at the sparse furnishings that helped hold down costs. As long as the rental was located within five miles of his favorite coffee chain, was spotlessly cleaned and the previous occupants hadn't smoked, Luke could be quite happy with used accommodations.

The thirty-eight-foot Praise Productions trailer afforded him the space to carry the few items he needed to be self-sufficient and comfortable during the weeks he'd spend at each location. Settling into a kitchen chair, he placed his morning latte on the table and dropped the newspaper beside it.

Four paws thumped the bedroom floor and Freeway lumbered around the corner. He stopped at the sight of his new master, wagged a long tail in a still-sleepy greeting and collapsed on the cool tile. His eyelids immediately sagged and he slipped back into puppy slumber.

Luke smiled at the contented animal and reached for the remote. Needing a quick feel for the local culture, he surfed dozens of Houston channels, pausing over the local television ministries.

Many of the services were in Spanish, leaving no doubt that the Hispanic population had exploded in Texas. A song recorded in Spanish would be a nice touch for the Harvest Sons album.

He reached for his backpack, pulled out a spiral notebook and pencil, and began making plans for the group. Though he wasn't willing to praise them too soon, last night the Sons had given one of the best first efforts Luke had observed so far. Eric was particularly hungry for success. After the taste Luke would offer the boy, he'd never settle for crumbs again. With youth and talent on his side he had a shot.

And now he had a secret weapon. Luke Dawson.

Seemed like only yesterday that Luke was just as trusting and hopeful. On his own at nineteen with enough money to do a world of good or a lot of damage, he lacked the maturity or the guidance to handle his fame. He'd naively signed over the management of his finances to entertainment lawyer Lisa Evans, never knowing he'd signed over full control as well. When a thick layer of dust settled on his career, she was a wealthy woman and he was lucky she'd left him the rights to his own music.

What different turns life might have taken if someone had stood in the gap for Luke Dawson before he became consumed by Striker Dark. He was committed to being that someone for Eric.

Since Luke had buried his anger along with Striker, he shook free of the memories and rattled open the Sunday paper.

The Southern Savage requires a Master. Do you have what it takes to dominate this machine?

The advertisement dared the reader. The rest of the full page ad listed the specs of the soon-to-be-released custom chopper, the signature bike of Savage Cycles of Houston.

Luke scanned the page for any mention of the owner. Finding none, he laid the paper on the table, folded his arms across his chest and squinted in concentration. Though he'd known her less than twenty-four hours, Claire Savage was possibly the most interesting woman he'd ever met. There was something apart from her physical beauty that demanded appreciation.

He found the self-confidence that bordered on arrogance appealing, and the matter-of-fact way she spoke of her accomplishments very attractive. Instead of the smug "I'm all that" kind of pride, she displayed a satisfied sureness that said she was capable and knew it.

There was no doubt she had a brilliant mind—the most worrisome part. After she'd left for the evening, Brian had offered a few unsolicited bits on her background. Seemed the mixture of pageant queen and Ivy League grad uniquely qualified her to serve as role model and femme fatale for the teens at Abundant Harvest. According to the boy, who was clearly smitten with her, the cool part was Claire didn't let all her achievements go to her head.

Luke recalled having the same foolish thoughts about Lisa when they'd first met. But something about this Miss Texas was different from the financial shark who had bled Striker Dark dry.

The way Claire held her head—chin just a bit high—was definitely practiced. But when he'd stared into her eyes he'd caught a glimmer of what lay beneath the public veneer. He wasn't sure it was confidence at all. He'd seen part bravado, part suspicion and something else. Fear maybe. Now what would a woman with the world by the tail have to fear?

She was a celebrity in this community, in this state actually. She had roots, an enviable past and was busy orchestrating a very public future. But he had a hunch she was afraid of something.

"Lord," Luke spoke aloud, "do me a favor, will Ya? Keep that woman busy with her own life and out of my hair?"

* * *

Claire closed her Bible and stood for the final prayer that would dismiss the worship service. She waited for the busy aisle to clear, and then made her way toward the exit. As she inched closer to the door she stopped to accept praise for her solo.

The arrangement was not one she'd personally have chosen but the song had complimented the series Pastor Ken was teaching on forgiveness. She'd agreed to sing the popular tune, hoping she wouldn't be compared unfavorably to the artist who'd won a Dove Award for the song. Though it bugged her to admit the truth, every suggestion Luke Dawson had imposed upon her last night had been right on target.

After following the instructions of a man who claimed he personally had the voice of a bullfrog, she'd found the comfort level that had been lacking when she'd practiced on her own. The guy was like that famous gymnastics coach who took the American women to the Olympics. He couldn't do a double back flip off the balance beam if his life depended on it, but the girls he trained never failed to bring home the gold.

Luke was nowhere to be found this morning, his rig no longer a conspicuous sight in the parking lot. A small sigh escaped as she realized she'd expected him to be there. She'd actually wanted the man's approval. She dropped her chin and trudged up the aisle.

"You were incredible this morning. Quite a moving performance."

Claire's head popped up as she recognized the male voice.

Arthur O'Malley stood just inside the exit door. In a lightweight summer suit, with his hands folded before him, he resembled a groom waiting for his bride.

Trained to accept a compliment graciously, this time she went with her gut instinct instead.

"Are you following me?" she demanded. "Because if you are you can kiss that interview goodbye."

His eyes flew wide, and a smile creased his face.

"Whoa, cowgirl," he chuckled. "I understand your stalker worries but this is just a coincidence. I'm staying right over there." He pointed to the luxury hotel across the interstate.

Her mother would have been appalled by the rude reaction. Good thing she was on an Alaskan cruise instead of standing beside her daughter. Still, something niggled at Claire, telling her to be cautious.

"I'm so sorry, Mr. O'Malley."

"It's Art." He waved away her formal address. "I'm on my way to Sunday brunch. Join me? We can take separate cars and even go Dutch treat if you'd prefer." He poked fun at her suspicious nature.

She'd skipped the past two meals and her stomach had mumbled its discontent throughout the sermon.

"I guess I can spare an hour." She accepted his invitation.

Minutes later, with Art's rented sedan visible in her rearview mirror, she pulled onto the access road and headed toward the restaurant they'd agreed upon. As she rolled to a stop at the intersection a familiar black rig turned in her direction. The driver's face was shielded by dark glasses and a baseball cap that was pulled low. But there was no mistaking Luke Dawson.

As the noisy diesel pickup passed, he glanced her way and seemed to dismiss her. She lifted her hand to wave but the moment was gone. Hunger forgotten, she regretted the lunch date and considered returning to the church.

A horn blared several cars back. Claire jumped, her attention snapping forward as the traffic light blinked from yellow to red. She twisted and mouthed an apology to Art.

Luke spotted the dazzling blonde in the pink Mustang.

How could anybody miss her in a car like that?

He shifted into second and pulled farther from the intersection. In the boxy rental directly behind her, a man smiled and waved. Though the gesture was obviously meant for Claire, Luke felt the motion like a punch to his belly.

After all these years, he was close enough to throw a rock at the gossip rag reporter who'd tracked

Striker Dark like a bounty hunter on the trail of an escaped convict. The guy who was currently a hot-shot with *Today's Times* would never be anything but a smarmy hack as far as Luke was concerned.

He snapped off the radio so he could concentrate. This day was bound to come. As carefully as he'd guarded his privacy, the world really was a small place. Sooner or later he'd be forced to cross paths with his past, but not today.

According to the digital clock on the dashboard the time was just after eleven. He could be packed and loaded in a couple of hours and make Austin or Dallas before supper. He reached for the travel-scarred canvas backpack on the seat beside him and fished inside for the Abundant Harvest contract. At the next convenience store he'd stop and use the payphone. Pastor Ken would have to deliver the news that Praise Productions regretfully was no longer free to work with the Harvest Sons.

The hopeful faces of Eric, Bryan, Zach and Chad invaded Luke's thoughts. He blinked twice to clear away the image of the four youths who'd been so eager to please. He batted away the heavy sense of responsibility he felt for Eric, the kid who needed a mentor, a protector and a father-figure as desperately as Luke himself once had.

Just twelve hours earlier they'd made a deal, and the boys had agreed to keep their end of the bargain. Luke had agreed a man's reputation was all he really had. He'd given them his word, said he never made a promise he couldn't keep. He'd prayed for discernment where Eric was concerned, asked God to guide his determination to make a difference in the boy's life.

Now Luke's shoulders slumped with the weight of how little his word would mean to the boys, to God.

In a week they'd remember the man who'd offered them the hope of a future as a fast talker who couldn't be trusted. He ground his teeth at the thought and stuffed the pages into the backpack.

"Lord, I don't know how all this figures into Your plan, but I can't run away this time." Luke accelerated as he passed the phone booth at the corner grocery. "I sure hope I don't regret this," he grumbled, and then headed for Abundant Harvest Church.

At 7:00 p.m. Claire leaned against the door with her shoulder and pushed her way into the church's narthex. The cardboard box in her hands was heavy with carry-out from her favorite Italian chain. Six to-go dinners would be her excuse for showing up again, and an assortment of jars from her mother's pantry would be an apology to Luke for her prank the night before.

After her brief lunch with O'Malley she'd spent the afternoon at the dealership pouring over the fine print of the Praise Production contact. Actually that wasn't true, because there was no fine print to speak of. The details of the agreement were short and specific, with no confusing clauses designed to hook the church into a bad deal. If Pastor Ken and his board voted to sign the document, she'd have no objections.

In fact, she was beginning to feel a bit guilty for her suspicions. Maybe her worry over the successful release of the Southern Savage was coloring other areas of her life.

The ad campaign that chewed up her entire marketing budget had begun that morning. In three weeks, the one-of-a-kind chopper would be loaded along with a dozen other bikes to begin the long journey to Sturgis, South Dakota. She was a woman invading a man's business. The future of Savage Cycles as a custom design shop would be riding along with the cargo.

There was no margin for error and no time to fix any. As usual, everything had to be perfect.

She sat the box on a table and pushed the sanctuary door open to peek inside. As he'd done the night before, Luke was quietly sharing some key points of music theory with the boys. Claire shook her head, amazed by the rapt attention on the faces of guys who would find this same lecture from their high school band director to be boring and pointless. When Luke paused to take a sip of his soft drink, she seized the opportunity to make her entrance.

"Anybody hungry?" she called.

"As long as it's not tacos I could sure use some supper," Luke responded, and turned with a ready smile so unexpected it rattled her self-control.

"If you'll settle for chicken parmesan I've got you covered." She propped the door wide, motioned for them to follow and then lifted the carton. Luke sprinted to catch up to her, taking the heavy box without discussion.

Claire nodded her thanks and dropped back to let him take the lead. She admired the solid shoulders beneath the black Praise Productions T-shirt and the trim waist where the shirt tucked loosely into his jeans. She straightened the floral scarf knotted at the neck of her pale yellow summer-weight sweater, and checked the length of her creased white Capri pants.

Glancing up, she locked eyes with Chad, who gave her a conspiratorial thumbs-up. She allowed the smallest smirk but narrowed her eyes in a "Don't go there" message.

Zach was the first to plop down at a table in the fellowship hall and help himself to a white carry-out container. He popped open the top and the aroma of marinara sauce floated above his meal.

He closed his eyes and sighed with obvious pleasure.

"Miss Claire, will you marry me?" he asked.

The boys snorted with agreeable laughter as they gathered around.

Claire looked at Brian, who was seated across the table from her, his head down over his meal.

"Will you bless the food for us, Brian?"

His eyes flew wide, and he shook his head.

"Mom's the only one who prays at our house." Eric explained his brother's reluctance.

"It's easy for men once we get some practice." Luke let the teen off the hook by offering sincere thanks for the meal. As they dug into their Italian carry-out, all conversation ceased. The teenage boys wolfed their food in record time and Luke excused them for the only cell phone check of the night, reminding them to call home. The two adults were left alone in the fellowship hall that felt huge and silent.

"Well, what's the verdict?" Luke caught her by surprise with the question. Did he somehow know she'd spent the previous night surfing the Net, searching for something that would prove his integrity? Or disprove it.

She paused, the plastic fork loaded with chicken and cheese halfway between the plate and her open mouth. The guy had great timing.

"Could you be more specific?" She stalled.

"Ken told me you'd be one of the folks checking the contract." He waited.

"I'm the head of the finance committee. It's my job to preview all monetary commitments to protect the church."

He spoke slowly, giving weight to each word as if addressing someone with trouble comprehending English.

"I repeat, what's the verdict? Did you find the 'gotcha' you were lookin' for?" He leveled her with his narrow gaze and casually bit into a garlic breadstick.

"No, I didn't find a single 'gotcha.'" The lightweight sweater was suddenly too warm. "I have no objections to the contract. It seems straightforward, exactly as you discussed it with Pastor Ken, so I gave the council my approval."

"Gee, thanks," he muttered. He looked down at his meal and resumed eating. It was perfectly reasonable for a church to have his contract reviewed before signing it, just as he should have done himself years ago. But for some reason it galled him that this woman acted like it was her personal mission to keep an eye on him.

"These are for you." She'd reached into the carryout carton and retrieved a brown paper sack. With a clunk, she deposited the bag on the table in front of him. He looked from the sack to her and back again.

"Go ahead," she insisted, waving her manicured hand toward the offering.

The opened sack revealed the tops of two pint-sized mason jars. He lifted one and then the other and felt a smile stretch across his face.

Jalapeños!

Chapter Five

"They're the painless kind. My mother grows them herself. She claims over-watering the plants and only using the smoothest peppers keeps them mild." Claire seemed to watch his face for approval.

"Go ahead, try one," she encouraged.

Enjoying the worry in her eyes over his acceptance of this peace offering, he thumped the edge of the lid on the table and twisted the cap. The seal broke with a light pop releasing the spicy scent. He tilted the open container her way.

"Ladies first."

As she might pick a delicate flower, she daintily plucked a stem between her thumb and forefinger. She tapped the dripping vinegar on the edge of the jar, raised the fiery fruit to her mouth and nibbled the edge. Eyes closed, she chewed and seemed to savor her mother's home-grown delicacy.

"Mmm, Mary Savage isn't the canning queen of Harris County for nothing." Claire dabbed at her lips with a paper napkin and grinned.

"Okay, I believe you." Luke nodded. "Mind if I save these for another occasion?" He replaced the lid with a secure twist.

"As long as you don't mind if I bring dinner every night and hang around to watch rehearsal."

"Don't you really mean hang around to watch me?"

"I beg your pardon." She squirmed a bit.

"You're determined to keep an eye on me, aren't you?" He couldn't seem to help himself. His professional motives were above reproach. But this lady still wasn't convinced.

"I admit there's some truth to that, but not entirely for the reason you think." She looked away and reached to gather the remnants of their meal. "The fact is you'll only be here a couple of weeks. These kids are like my family and I already see the hero worship on their faces when they look at you. They'll need someone to fill the void in their lives when you're gone. Especially Eric and Brian. Things are rough at that house. I may not be anybody's first choice but I could be all they have until somebody else steps up."

She stopped her busy work of wiping down the table and looked him in the eye. "So, if you don't mind, I'd like to learn everything I can while you're here."

His chest tightened at the brutal honesty of her statement. How many times had he driven away from youngsters who'd begged him to stay longer? Determined to be in control of his own destiny, he'd packed up and moved on. And he'd almost walked away again just a few hours earlier.

He shrugged off the internal nagging and turned the recrimination he deserved on her instead.

"I guess I don't mind," he groused. "As a matter of fact, I almost admire that streak of meddling do-gooder in you."

Her hand brushed the cross around her neck as her brown eyes widened at the barely veiled insult. Would he never learn to control the mouth that had earned him countless backhands from his Naval officer father?

"That was unfair," Luke muttered a near apology.

"It's okay. I know I need to disguise it a little better." She flushed slightly at the admission and he felt like even more of a jerk.

"Speaking of meddling, I can probably find a permanent home for Freeway when you leave. I already have three foster animals but I'll make room for one more at my little place for a while."

The woman he'd just offended was offering to help him out. Turning the other cheek, as the Bible taught. Something he'd never mastered. He mentally shrunk to the height of a rotted tree stump and felt about as useful.

The way his mouth pinched into a thin line told Claire she'd struck a nerve. Nice to see the guy cared about something besides music.

"Thanks, but no." He gave an adamant shake of his head. "I promised Freeway he could stay with me."

"And you never make a promise…" She paused.

He tilted his head in the same way Tripod and Buck did when they were trying to make sense of her babbling.

"You don't intend to keep," she quoted him. "I overheard you tell the boys that last night. I was eavesdropping as any meddling do-gooder worth her salt would." She winked, a confirmation he was forgiven, then reached for the box of trash.

He waved her hand away, hefted the carton of trash himself, and turned toward the door that led outside to the Dumpster. When he returned she casually confirmed their agreement.

"So you don't mind if I stick around?"

He deposited quarters in the soda machine and selected two drinks known for their high caffeine content. This would be another long night.

"On two conditions."

She nodded, ready to go along with just about anything.

"One, don't interfere. I may seem rough with them sometimes, but there's always a method to my madness."

"That's fair enough. And two?"

He flashed a sheepish grin. "Give me a preview of that new bike of yours."

"You ride?"

"Never had time to learn. Besides, I'm kinda partial to four wheels between me and the concrete. But you're obviously a thrill-seeker, right?"

She only answered that question when she had no choice. Otherwise she avoided it like the chicken pox.

"Nope." She made the admission, turned about-face and headed for the sanctuary.

Claire was impressed by the staff that accompanied Arthur O'Malley's Monday visit to Savage Cycles. The freelance photographer that she'd envisioned would snap a few photos and be on his way, turned out to be a double camera crew capable of stills and video depending on the opportunity, not to mention a producer to direct the shots. It seemed *Today's Times* left nothing to chance, even taping clips for their cable news show as the situation allowed.

A pro before an audience, Claire made easy work of waiting on customers, giving the shop tour and explaining the unique design behind the Southern Savage while O'Malley and two photographers followed her every move.

As she had a thousand times during her public

life, she wondered if the man who had soiled her childhood would be among those who'd see her pictures. The thought made her flesh crawl, but at least she didn't fear he'd do anything to reveal her shame. He'd been silent for well over a decade, and she knew the coward would remain that way for a lifetime.

"I have to 'fess up to something," Claire confided once she and Art were settled alone in her office for the interview. "I haven't read the 'Out of the Spotlight' feature in several years. When that Olympic triathlete who'd spent most of his life in and out of rehab hospitals was exposed, I decided those stories weren't for me."

Art accepted the soft drink she offered him, settled it on the table beside his chair and uncapped a gold monogrammed pen.

"Then why did you agree to do this?"

She glanced down, politely cleared her throat behind her hand and finally met his eyes.

"Money." She was blunt.

"Ahh, the great motivator." He nodded.

"I investigated the cost of national advertising. There was no way I could afford the campaign I wanted to do. I've sunk most of my budget into newspaper marketing and the rest is earmarked for the Sturgis bike rally."

"So my arrival two days ago was actually a good thing." He held his soda aloft in a salute.

She raised her drink and prayed the sinking feeling in her stomach wasn't an omen she'd live to regret.

The afternoon passed smoothly as Claire shared her journey from teen titles to graduate school to entrepreneurship. She lightly skimmed over her trip to the Miss America finals but took time to dispel the common myth that behind every beauty queen is a stage-struck mama. Mary Savage had been anything but a pushy woman living vicariously through her child. Together they'd strategically selected and prepared for each competition with Claire's educational goals uppermost in mind. Yes, it had been a life of sacrifice and discipline, but the end justified the means.

The intercom on her desk beeped to signal Justin was transferring an important call. Art glanced down and discretely reviewed his notes as Claire took a moment to confirm her special-order parts would be shipped by overnight express.

"I'm sorry for the interruption," she apologized. "But I've been holding my breath for that information. We took a chance on an independent parts distributor. He's had trouble delivering our order and I refuse to use a foreign vendor."

"Tell me more about your American-only policy?"

Claire warmed to the subject of American-made products, something she'd focused on during her months in graduate school.

"I take it you won't have any objection to *Today's Times* using your position on this subject as a central theme in the article."

"Not as long as that theme is flanked by an opening and closing mention of the Southern Savage's unveiling in Sturgis." She emphasized her priority hoping her opinion mattered. Claire realized her drive to see her project succeed could be the closest she'd ever come to parental pride. She was determined to enjoy every baby step along the way.

"Miss Claire's in the parking lot and there's a camera crew with her!" Zach shouted.

Luke watched as the kid tossed his head, giving his dark curls that freshly mussed look the girls seemed to love. Zach was a natural entertainer, always aware of his potential audience.

"For real?" Chad's voice cracked with the question, his eyes wider than usual behind his black horn-rims.

"Come see for yourself." Zach headed back through the door he'd left standing open behind him.

All heads turned toward Luke for approval.

"Go on, take five," he grudgingly acquiesced. "But shut the door," he called as the three sprinted up the aisle, followed by the few volunteers who were painting a backdrop for the upcoming week of vacation Bible school.

"Just what we needed," Luke muttered, "a distraction right before our audition. It figures Miss Texas would parade a media circus through here when those guys really need to focus."

Even as he grumbled, Luke felt certain the Harvest Sons would get the nod to continue the impressive progress of the past two days. The council would be arriving any minute and the boys were eager to the point of being antsy. A brief diversion would probably do them good.

Ken had given Luke a videotape of their amateurish Battle of the Bands performance. They'd open up with that video on the jumbo screens overhead and then hit the darkened stage with a filtered spot as the Sons launched into an up-tempo version of the same tune. The musical evidence of their improvement would speak volumes.

Deciding to stick around had definitely been the right thing to do. These kids had special promise and Praise Productions was going to give them the recording that would launch them onto the professional music scene. But he couldn't seem to get Claire's comments from the night before out of his head. A sense of worry niggled at him over eventually leaving the Sons to fend for themselves.

"Hey, Luke," Ken Allen called.

Luke smiled, in an odd way relieved by the presence of the pastor, who felt more like a personal friend than a church leader.

"Our middle schoolers hang out here on Monday

nights and I invited them to the show. Looks like you're gonna have quite an audience, so I hope you don't mind."

"Fine by me." Luke enjoyed the thought of a crowd to pump the guys up. "They'll be more comfortable playing to a room full of kids than a dozen adults anyway."

"And you won't be bothered by the film crew?" Pastor Ken scrunched his face in a silent appeal.

Luke's skin grew warm beneath his dark shirt and he fought the desire to shove the long sleeves up to his elbows. He'd managed to stay away from cameras since he'd been twenty-five. There were more than enough photos of him out there to last a lifetime.

"I guess not," he agreed, "as long as all the attention is on the band. If the Sons expect to be more than garage musicians they'll have to get used to cameras."

"Thanks, Luke. That's what I figured you'd say."

Fifteen minutes later, Luke found himself in the middle of a school bus driver's worst nightmare. The room was alive with obnoxious middle schoolers. Boys showed off for girls who wouldn't give them a second glance. Voices competed for attention and the rubber tips of folding chairs screeched against the wooden floor as kids jockeyed for the front-row seats. The adults kept a safe distance, forming a tight huddle near the middle of the room.

Truth be told, the environment was perfect to preview the band's new sound. If the Sons could capture this rowdy group's attention, the adults would follow like lost sheep. Luke caught the pastor's eye and gave a wave of approval. The two men exchanged nods, as if sharing the same thought.

The room went black as video flickered to life on the two oversized screens. The kids continued to chatter, their notice divided between the music overhead and the band moving into position behind their instruments on the darkened stage.

From his bird's eye view inside the A/V booth, Luke noted the stealth entrance of a woman and several men, two of them carrying camera equipment. Even in the dark there was no mistaking Claire's platinum blond hair and perfect posture.

The video timer counted backward.

Five, four, three, two, one.

"Show time," Luke spoke into the mic that carried his voice into each musician's tiny headset.

Eric launched into the opening riff and Luke hit the spot, illuminating the four in streams of crisp white light. Eric's raspy vocals blasted from the amps and the crowd of young teens jumped to their feet. Unable to contain their enthusiasm, the adults followed suit.

Luke made no effort to control the satisfied smile that spread across his face. This was the best part, maybe even better than the performance that produced the recording. In the past forty-eight hours, these extraordinary young men had begun to understand their true potential. This moment, when a musician feels the power of the gift, was the reason Luke stuck with his life-on-the-move existence.

The arrangement had been extended to give each member of the group time for a brief solo but not long enough to detract from the message of the music. A key Praise Production goal was the focus on the Word, making sure the spiritual theme wasn't lost in the rock beat.

His strategy worked. The house lights came up, the kids swarmed the stage like ants to a picnic lunch and the church council turned toward the sound booth to applaud their approval. The three teen volunteers in the booth with Luke cheered.

"They were radical!" Dana, in punk mode for the evening, was clearly wowed by the performance of the boys she idolized.

Luke beamed at the girl who couldn't have been more excited if she'd been on the stage herself.

"I think we're gonna need some help for a couple of weeks, Dana. How about joining us?"

Budding self-confidence colored the face of the otherwise insecure girl, whose eyes telegraphed her raw need to fit in.

"If you're sure…I don't want to be in the way." She ducked her head and fiddled with a toggle switch as she waited for his response.

Pastor Ken pushed open the door. "Luke, come on out. We're unanimous and ready to sign on the dotted line."

"Be with y'all shortly."

Ken turned and let the door close quietly.

Luke spoke softly to the girl. "I've watched you set the mics and monitor the board. You're a natural. We need you on our team."

She glanced up as he sent her a look of open approval. Her nod of agreement put several pair of hoop earrings into motion. He had himself another stray.

Luke joined the pastor, accepted congratulations and tucked the signed document under his arm.

Two weeks. He'd just committed himself to two more weeks at Abundant Harvest Church. He'd book a recording session by Wednesday and have the selections nailed down by Friday. If everybody worked as hard as they had over the weekend, two weeks would be more than enough time.

"Hey, Luke, do you have a minute?"

He turned toward the question, an unexpected spark of pleasure surging through his chest at the sound of Claire's voice.

Chapter Six

The warmth of Luke's smile brushed Claire's face like the rays of a Texas summer sun. A moment later his attention flickered over her shoulder and in short order his sunny look of accomplishment clouded over with dark annoyance.

"I have someone I'd like you to meet." She forged ahead despite his glower.

"Bad timing, Miss Texas. I'm conducting business in case you hadn't noticed." He turned his back, disregarding her completely.

Though they'd parted on a note of agreement the night before, she wasn't so naive as to expect a personal welcome today. Still, her efforts to include the Harvest Sons in the magazine fanfare deserved some positive response from Luke. Didn't it? But based on this reaction to the *Today's Times* crew, she'd obviously misjudged the value of her surprise.

Unaccustomed to being snubbed, Claire felt the heat of anger rise in her cheeks.

"It's okay, son. There's time enough tomorrow to wrap up the details." Pastor Ken stepped around Luke and covered the moment of rudeness. Ken took over the introductions, extending his hand to the newcomer.

"I'm Ken Allen, the senior pastor here."

"Pastor Ken—" She hesitated, toying for a moment with the idea of ignoring Luke completely. "And Luke Dawson, I'd like to introduce Arthur O'Malley of *Today's Times* Magazine."

Luke turned, watched Ken and Art exchange comments about the band's performance, then tucked his chin and inched away from the circle of light that surrounded them. When he glanced up, his lips were pressed into that tight line she'd seen several times. Claire wanted to shrink from the aggravation on his face but she stood tall.

Ken excused himself to rejoin the council. Art motioned for the cameras to wait for him at the door and then turned to Luke.

"Pleased to meet you, Luke. We got some great footage of the audition and we'd like to get a few stills of Claire and the youngsters she sings with if you don't mind."

Luke avoided any possibility of a handshake by grabbing the contract and rolling it into a tight paper tube, as he turned toward the stage.

"Nope. No time for publicity tonight," he said, refusing the request. "We have real work to do."

Claire clenched her fists at his abrupt dismissal. She could wring Luke's ornery neck.

"Well…" Art politely retreated. "Maybe tomorrow, then. I can come back when you're not so pressed for time. From what Claire tells me you have quite an impressive setup. Maybe our entertainment editor would be interested in doing a piece on you."

Luke jerked his head toward Art. There was no denying the message in Luke's eyes. He made no effort to disguise the pure, unadulterated disgust.

"No thanks, hotshot. Use the band to help out Miss Savage all you want, but my work speaks for itself." He turned on his heel and strode toward the mass of middle schoolers that still dominated the front of the sanctuary.

"Luke!" Claire gasped. She was embarrassed to the core by the uncalled-for surly behavior. Determined to give him a piece of her mind, she took two steps in his direction. Art caught her arm, stopping her progress.

She yanked her arm free of his touch.

"Sorry!" Art insisted. His eyes were round, his palms raised and spread declaring his innocence. "I didn't mean to startle you, just let you know you don't need to bother with Dawson. It's okay if he's not interested."

She glanced from Luke's rigid back to Art's wide eyes, a loud sigh voicing her exasperation.

"And don't give his comment another thought." He angled his head toward Luke. "If I got my feelings hurt over the way some people react to the press I'd spend a lot of time in the fetal position."

"Still..." She risked a quick look toward Luke. He was engaged in conversation with the teens, seemingly oblivious to her feelings, never giving her the time to explain her intentions.

"Hey, thanks for letting us interrupt your day."

She pried her gaze away and turned to Art.

"I'm the one who should be thanking you for this opportunity. The timing couldn't be more perfect." She followed him up the aisle toward the exit. "Any chance I'll get to preview the article before it goes to print?"

"Sorry, no. My editor makes the final changes and at that point deadlines are tight. But I'll fax an advance copy to you before the issue hits the stands."

The crew headed for their cars in the parking lot and Claire stood alone for a moment, praying for the right way to address Luke's behavior. She'd only known him a few days, but she'd witnessed a dozen flashes of kindness and generosity slip though his gruff exterior. She was clearly being drawn to him but hadn't the slightest idea why she should respond to those emotions. His lifestyle certainly precluded any relationship potential and he wasn't the easiest guy to deal with.

Still, she sensed a painful need within Luke. A pain she understood and possibly a need she could help fill.

But the fact remained that ten minutes ago he'd been coarsely out of line, behavior she'd long refused to tolerate from any man.

Young voices drifted down the hall as the preteens returned to their planned activities. The council was meeting in the church study, leaving only the Harvest Sons and Luke in the sanctuary. Ignoring the good sense of letting a little more time dull her anger, she made a beeline for the spot where he rested in a folding chair, his head down over the spiral notebook in his hands.

Luke recognized the busy cadence that always accompanied her approach, so there was no need to look up to know who was bearing down on him.

"Just answer one question for me," Claire demanded.

His gaze shifted from the list of potential song titles to the pointy-toed shoes she wore. The right shoe *tap-tap-tapped* her impatience. Tonight she was a vision in pink, from the rose-colored heels to her identically matching and sharply creased slacks, topped by a blouse the exact hue of her flushed cheeks.

A couple of times now he'd seen her in a dither, her fists positioned on her hips. He witnessed that stance before him now. But instead of bracing for what was coming, he allowed himself to enjoy the image of perfection whose attention was his alone. An odd tingling of pleasure that he hadn't experienced in many years swamped his senses.

"Are you a one-man show because you're too proud to share the spotlight or because you're so rude that nobody will stand in it next to you?" Her caramel eyes were narrowed, telegraphing the fact that he was the singular focus of her annoyance.

He had a reprimand coming but didn't intend to accept it just yet. "Is there any chance there's a third choice that's a little less incriminating?"

A woman on a power trip would have continued to tower over him. Claire dropped to the chair beside him and puffed out a breath to move the bangs off the tips of her long lashes.

"What was that all about, Luke?" Her voice lost its demanding tone, but the storm in her eyes said she expected an answer.

"I might ask you the same thing. You knew what was at stake tonight. Did you think about that before you decided to show up at the last minute with your entourage?"

She slumped a bit in her chair. "Art was at the dealership all afternoon because *Today's Times* is doing a feature on Savage Cycles. I invited them to come along, thinking you'd appreciate some potential publicity for Praise Productions and the Sons."

"Did it occur to you to ask first?"

"I did," she insisted. "I phoned Pastor Ken before I said anything to Art."

Luke recalled Ken's mention of the film crew and knew she spoke the truth. But instead of apologizing for jumping to conclusions, he locked onto another subject.

"No-oo-o, we wouldn't want to offend Aa-aa-art," he singsonged. "Isn't he about a decade too old for you?"

She cocked an eyebrow at the wisecrack that made him sound like a jealous boyfriend.

"Not that it's any of your business, but he seems like a nice guy. And it's worth the risk of letting the press into my life if his column helps me launch the Savage."

"Worth the risk?" he repeated, more curious about her than ever.

The woman who was so big on eye contact dropped her gaze, fiddled with her cross. Her bravado slipped. She had something at risk, something private. A subject he knew a lot about. A true stage professional, she slid behind her mask of perfect composure and met his stare.

"Oh, you know reporters. Writing about your business life is never enough. Sooner or later they want personal details, but that's where I draw the line."

And, he guessed, there must be a good reason for that.

"Since I ran off sugar daddy…"

She raised a clenched fist in fair warning.

"Are you going to leave mad or stick around again to keep an eye on me?" he continued. "I've officially picked up a stray kid, and I think she could use some female influence."

Luke turned in the direction of the A/V booth. The silhouette of the girl's spiked hair was recognizable through the dark glass. Claire must have spotted her.

"You mean our Dana?" A soft sigh accompanied the question. "That poor kid is really struggling to know who she wants to be."

"I'd settle for her figuring out who she is right now," Luke insisted. "She looks like a different person every time I see her. I have a good memory for faces and I've introduced myself to her three times already."

"Well, she has an ultra-conservative Texas Ranger daddy and she's never known her mama so there's no woman in her life. Dana definitely changes her fashion statement from one day to the next, but her faith is the common thread in all her styles. She may be mixed up, but she's certain of the one thing that matters most. So she spends a bunch of time at Abundant Harvest, where we all accept her and love her."

Like a river overflowing its banks, longing spilled over Luke. Unconditional welcome must be nice. A kid could get away with that, but an adult had to earn the approval and respect of his peers. And it was tiring work, a day-to-day existence.

He slapped the notebook on the floor, tightened the laces of his worn-out All Stars, rose to his feet and shoved his hands deep into his pockets. "So, what's it gonna be? You hanging around or bailing out tonight?"

"Nice try, but you haven't completely thrown me off course." She stood, adjusted the shoulder strap of the leather bag that matched her shoes and nailed him with a determined stare.

"Luke, you embarrassed me in front of those people. It may be your style to do everything solo, but I'm in the business of selling rather expensive toys. I need all the positive promotion and clients I can get."

"Fair enough." He hesitated, not sure he was prepared for what he was about to do. Outside of an introduction or sealing a deal, he hadn't made a physical overture to a woman in years. But as if his right hand had a will of its own, it slipped from the comfort of his denim pocket and reached toward Claire, an offering of peace.

Could she accept the mixed-up stuff that was his world just as she'd done for the troubled girl in the sound booth?

The smile that must have earned her trophies and tiaras curved her pale pink lips and crinkled the corners of her mesmerizing eyes. His heart thudded beneath his black T-shirt as she slipped her small, warm hand into his. And just like the first time, she seemed in no hurry to be free of his touch.

Claire felt a strange lightness in her soul, as they bonded through the simple handshake that he'd seemed to consider for ages before his muscles engaged. There was a reason why the number of people she made voluntary physical contact with could be counted on one hand.

But at this moment the permanent bruises from her childhood were a distant thought, deep below the surface of calm waters. For the first time in her life she understood why a woman would want to be drawn into a man's embrace.

The warmth that had passed from his hand to hers leapt straight to her heart. If she didn't break the contact soon he'd recognize her racing pulse in her touch. Worse still, he'd feel the nervous dampness that was breaking through her palm at that moment.

As if he sensed discomfort looming, Luke eased the light pressure of his grip giving her the cue she needed to slip her hand out of his and rotate her wrist to check her watch.

"It's dinnertime and those guys need something to soak up all that soda they're chugging." She glanced toward the grinning boys, who saluted one another with drink cans in celebration of their triumph.

"My stomach couldn't agree more." Luke patted

his midsection then gave her a hopeful look. "Have I blown it so bad that our only dinner option is Dana's sack of fried Spam sandwiches?"

Claire couldn't help but grin at the way his eyebrows rose as he pleaded his case. The guy was really quite charming when he forgot about that chip on his shoulder.

"I think Spam will compliment the pizza and salads I ordered very nicely."

He turned and cupped his hands to his mouth, megaphone-style. "Hey guys, Miss Claire's gonna hang around again tonight and help us out."

They gave four thumbs-up to the announcement and Luke raised his shoulders and eyebrows in a there-you-go shrug.

"Actually, I arranged for the restaurant to deliver tonight. I have an early commitment in the morning and I thought I'd give you a break this evening. I know how you feel about my meddling."

A flicker of sadness darkened his forest-green eyes for a moment, and her heart swelled the tiniest bit. The grouch who'd dismissed her presence less than an hour ago actually seemed disappointed by her decision to call it an early night.

"Why stop now when I'm getting used to it?" he asked. "Besides, I was counting on you to help out with Dana."

Secretly delighted by the unexpected emotion on his face, she resolved to stick to her plan. Showing off with a flashy turn in front of a judge who was already in your corner was never a good idea. Mama had taught her the best time to leave the stage was when the crowd was cheering for more.

That was sound advice in all aspects of life.

"Give me a rain check. There are plenty of volunteers around tonight and Dana will do just fine under your considerate tutelage," Claire said with a roll of her eyes, then turned to leave.

But she was only half-mocking. Luke's guidance at the soundboard was the perfect thing to boost the girl's suffering self-esteem, and Ken would always make sure there was another adult around.

Tonight she would wrap up her long day with a cool shower followed by a peanut butter and banana sandwich shared with Buck, R.C. and Tripod. With the heat expected to rise above 100 degrees in the shade, tomorrow would be even longer.

Claire slid into the leather seat of her pony car, her feelings a jumble from the day's events. She'd cooperated with Arthur O'Malley and there was no turning back. In a few days, her name would appear in hundreds of thousands of copies of *Today's Times* magazine. The exposure meant incredible publicity for Savage Cycles, but she couldn't help feeling she'd sold out on some level. Given up something she could never get back.

And then there was her confusion over Luke. One moment he was as set in his ways as any cantankerous old curmudgeon, but the next his words and actions were aglow with his faith. He had a pure heart for the work he did with young musicians and he couldn't hide his light under a bushel no matter how hard he tried.

As Claire pulled out of the parking lot and headed for home, she said a prayer of thanks because she felt a little closer to understanding what made Luke Dawson tick.

Chapter Seven

At eight forty-five the next morning, Luke pulled into his now-familiar corner of the Abundant Harvest parking lot. He tucked keys in his front pocket, grabbed his cup of coffee and slammed the pickup door. Four hours of sleep weren't nearly enough for a full day of chaperone duty. But when the pastor had stopped by last evening looking to draft Luke, Ken simply wouldn't take "no" for an answer. The middle school group needed one more adult for their trip to Houston's family amusement park and unless Luke personally volunteered they'd have to cancel. Luke wasn't about to risk the kids' excursion by insisting he had work of his own to do, so with a grunt and a scowl he'd signed the pastor's clipboard and sent Ken on his way with a smug smile on his face.

Just to make sure the day wasn't a total productivity loss, Luke had insisted the Harvest Sons make the trip with him. At the very least they'd talk through their plans and practice some vocals a cappella. There was a smattering of objection until Luke mentioned he was the hands-free, roller coaster champion who intended to defend his title on the Cyclone. Once the challenge was issued all four boys took the bait. Now Luke just had to find some food to soak up the coffee in his stomach or he'd be tossing his cookies during the ride's first eighty-foot drop.

He hiked across asphalt that was still simmering from the previous day's heat. His jeans and black T-shirt would make it easy for the kids to spot him in the barely dressed summer crowd. He tugged the bill of his favorite Braves cap, adjusted dark glasses that hid his eyes and put on his best brooding expression. Maybe if he looked sinister and imposing they'd cower in fear. Fat chance.

Through the windows of the recycled commuter bus Luke could see the squirming youngsters who were too hopped up on sugary cereal to sit still. Once they got a belly full of cotton candy and funnel cakes their blood sugar would be off the charts. The adolescent diet made Luke shudder, but he figured a glucose high was small beans compared to the stuff he'd put in his body when he wasn't much older.

The bus driver cranked open the door and Luke was relieved to feel a whoosh of cool air. He stomped up the three metal steps, turned to the left and prepared to glare into the faces of unsuspecting preteens.

"Well, good morning." The voice was a welcome melody. Eyes like warm caramel glinted with humor. "What a nice surprise." Claire flashed her beauty queen smile as she slid toward the window and offered him the aisle seat beside her.

He dropped down to the Naugahyde bench and squeezed himself into the space designed for a much shorter person. Looking over at Claire he noted her long legs were angled to make the most of what little space was available. And, as always, she was beautifully put together in those chopped-off jean things and a white cotton shirt with rolled-up cuffs. Her hair was bunched up on top of her head with a gold clip and small diamond earrings flashed in the morning sunlight.

"I thought you had an early commitment," he grumbled.

"This is it."

"You got drafted yesterday too, huh?" He slumped as low as space would allow and propped his knees against the seat in front.

"Actually, I volunteered over a month ago without realizing how busy things would be at the shop this week. We're taking inventory and I really should be working with my parts manager on what we're shipping to Sturgis, but I couldn't let these kids down."

He slipped off the dark shades and let them dangle by a braided chord around his neck. He folded his arms, resting them against his chest and turned to the stunning woman beside him. When he spoke his voice was low, his words sincere.

"I know you're proud of your talents for business and music, but I think your kind heart is probably your greatest natural gift."

"Why, thank you, Luke." She blushed like one of the seventh-grade girls.

"Can I ask you a personal question, Claire?"

"Sure." She nodded.

"When do you make time for yourself?"

"I could ask you the same thing." She turned the tables without answering. "You've spent a lot of hours here in the past few days."

"Yeah, and I'm being compensated for my time."

"You're not on the payroll today, so what are you doing on this bus?"

He drew his eyebrows together and considered her question.

"See?" She enjoyed a self-satisfied smile. "You have a pretty soft heart yourself, Luke. You think you have it buried so deep no one will notice, but my guess is you're all bark and no bite." Several kids giggled at her assessment.

The driver stood and gave final orders for the kids to take a seat, and to hold the volume down.

Luke slipped his glasses back in place and covered a wide yawn with his palm. Then he spoke in a menacing voice as he glanced around, "Boys and girls, better listen to the man. I'm gonna take a little nap and the first kid who wakes me will get to put Miss Claire's theory about my bite to the test." He tossed his empty paper cup into the driver's trash can, pulled his cap low and dropped his chin to his chest.

He pressed his eyes shut but couldn't miss the crackling sound as Claire rustled a paper sack. The aroma of cinnamon tickled his nose and, without moving a muscle, he cracked one eye open to see what tempted his senses. She unwrapped a fat scone, broke off the corner and popped the pastry into her mouth.

Claire heard Luke's stomach growl loud enough to solicit more giggles from the girls across the aisle. She leaned close and caught him peeking over his sunglasses, eyeing her breakfast. She broke off another large bite, lifted it close and inhaled the spicy scent.

"Mmm," she expressed her pleasure before nibbling the edge of the sweet biscuit.

His stomach complained again and he shifted in the seat to disguise the rumbling. She reached into the bag, pulled out another cinnamon-and-raisin scone and held it under his nose.

"You interested?"

"Since you asked." Luke let the glasses slip off

his face and fastened his gaze with hers. "I'm very interested. In fact, more than my good sense dictates."

She stared into his unreadable eyes, not sure how to respond. Was he making an overture or just a joke?

"But we're with a busload of kids right now, so I'll settle for your extra scone if that's a bona fide offer."

Now it was her turn for the stomach flutters. She covered her nervousness by rifling the sack for napkins and then handing over the pastry.

"You've been feeding me for three solid days. How about letting me buy you dinner tonight for a change?" He switched subjects before sinking even, white teeth into the freshly baked confection and moaning his gratitude. She popped the lid off her cup and he accepted a sip of black coffee.

"What do you say, Claire? Chili cheese dogs and curly fries from the food court? One of my favorite meals of all time." He winked and gave her the short version of his lazy smile before turning his focus to the remainder of his scone. "Is it a date?" he asked casually, probably knowing his question was so nonchalant that later he could pretend he'd been joking and get away with it.

"Sure," she accepted.

She'd had more sophisticated meal proposals in recent weeks and rejected them all to spend the evening with her pets. But the thought of sharing a greasy meal with Luke Dawson at an amusement park food court was more appealing than any date at a five-star restaurant.

Appealing and dangerous. Both the company *and* the food.

The Cyclone was a 65 mile-per-hour adrenaline rush for a veteran thrill-junkie. But for the novice the wooden masterpiece could be two minutes of pure terror.

"You're going to love it," Luke cajoled. "Now come on and sit down." He patted the seat beside him.

The kids had begged her to make the ride with them. After the long wait in line he'd figured she'd be up for it, but trepidation was etched into her classic features. Her normally rosy lips were white with tension. The tiny laugh lines at the corners of her lovely eyes were deep with worry, and if she didn't stop fiddling with her cross she'd snap the spindly chain.

"Why don't I just wait here for y'all?" She tried for a lighthearted sound but her voice trembled in time with her hands.

For a moment he considered letting her off the hook, but the appeal of having this enticing, shivering female next to him for the short duration of the ride was too much to resist. He offered up a silent prayer of apology for the selfish act he was about to commit.

"No way." He held out his hand to steady her step down into the rickety-feeling car. "Let's go, you're holding up the line."

Her cheeks puffed out with the air she exhaled and she gripped his fingers and hopped onto the seat. She squeezed his hand with surprising strength, refusing to let go. His head told him it was an unconscious act but his racing heart hoped otherwise.

"Way to go, Miss Claire!" Zach yelled, and the Abundant Harvest youth who had packed the train called out their approval. The metal bars locked securely across their laps and the noisy cart began to creep forward at a slug's pace.

Claire squeezed her eyes shut and pressed her side as tightly to Luke's as decency would allow. "I don't know why I let you taunt me into this. There's a reason why I don't ride my own choppers and you're looking at it! If my hair turns gray I'll never forgive you, Luke Dawson!"

Luke's chest ached over her pitiful effort to joke. Her trembling was reaching the panic stage and they hadn't even left the platform.

"Ladies and gentlemen," the ride operator called over the loud speaker. "You are about to experience the awesome power of the most dangerous twister known to mankind...the Cyclone!"

Youthful cheering blended with a high-pitched

screech as wheels engaged for the trip uphill. This wooden wonder wasn't propelled by a motor or pulled by a hitch. Only pure kinetic energy would be in control once the coaster descended the first hill.

"Hold tight to the restraining bar—" the operator paused for whoops of refusal "—and I'll see *most* of you back here in two minutes and fifteen seconds." The train began to chug up the steep incline in earnest, forcing the riders back against the seats.

Claire's nails dug into Luke's fingers.

"Ouch," he yelped.

"Don't you dare complain," she threatened through gritted teeth, her voice muffled where she pressed her face against his shoulder. "I don't care if you bleed or end up with permanent bruises. This is scarring me mentally for life, so prepare to suffer along with me."

Luke twisted his left arm free of her grasp, lifted it over her head and laid it around her, a shield against her fears. He pulled her close and angled his face down to the top of her platinum blond head. Without a thought for the impropriety or consequences, he brushed a kiss against her crown. The touch was the most foreign yet natural thing he'd ever done. And he was repaid for his intimacy by an ear-splitting scream.

Claire was certain her lungs would burst from the force of the wail that accompanied every inch of the eighty-foot drop. She gripped the metal safety bar with one hand and clutched Luke's shirt front with the other. She'd wriggled her right shoe between Luke's big sneakers and anchored herself to his feet. She was vaguely aware that her face was cradled between his shoulder and chin.

Being halfway into his lap was the least of her worries. What difference did it make how things looked when she was about to die of fright? She alternately pleaded with Luke and God for help. If Luke's arms weren't strong enough to hold her at least she was certain God would ultimately catch her.

She'd known more than a few fearful times in her life. Moments filled with terror, days of dread, frightening experiences stepping from the predictable to the unknown. But the physical panic that accompanied what these people considered "fun" was beyond all reason. If she could have stood up she'd have kicked herself!

Why had she agreed to do this in the first place? The car took a steep turn and rocked precariously from side to side, giving the intentional impression it was close to leaving the track. She snaked both arms around Luke's waist and buried her face against his chest.

Luke Dawson!

He was the reason she was in this life and death situation! If not for his coaxing and teasing she'd be standing on blessed concrete, not rushing through space with nothing but a wooden washtub between her and eternity. Luke was to blame. Luke was dirt.

Luke was muttering something into her hair. Claire was tempted to look up and ask him to repeat himself but the track suddenly dropped out from under them and the train nosedived for the earth. She wanted to scream but the sound was lodged in her chest. Her heart beat with such fury she wondered if her body could survive it. She held tight and listened to the throbbing of her pulse in her ears.

But she suddenly realized the pounding wasn't in her head at all, but beneath the surface she clutched for dear life. The thumping she felt was Luke's heart, matching hers beat for beat. Was the big jerk as frightened as she was?

No way. He'd boasted of being the hands-free roller coaster champion. He was here to defend his title against guys half his age and that challenge was issued last night before he ever knew she'd be there. No, his heart wasn't hammering because of fear at all.

Now that she'd refocused her attention on Luke she was aware of how he held her, snug against his chest with both strong arms wrapping her in a protective embrace. Her head was tucked beneath his chin and he muttered soothing sounds into her hair. Had he planned this all along?

She should push away and ram her elbow in his

ribs for setting her up, but two things held her back. The first was the centrifugal force that had her pinned against Luke like a bug to a windshield. The second was another force that she suspected was even more powerful.

The pleasure of his embrace.

The days were getting longer and the fireworks weren't scheduled to start until nine. At 7:00 p.m., the kids begged to stay for the show and the bus driver said he didn't mind hanging around till the park closed. So, once again, Luke had to go along or be the bad guy.

Everybody enjoyed a fireworks display and he was no exception, so he'd agreed. There was a day when he'd been mesmerized by the choreographed pyrotechnics that ended his band's outdoor concerts. Great cannons launched missiles into the black sky that exploded into rainbow showers of sparks. He'd watched along with his young fans, amazed at the science that produced the spectacular light shows. As misguided as Striker had been, there were times when he'd reacted like the normal kid that he was deep inside. Luke was grateful that God allowed the occasional flash of insight into that confusing time in his life.

"Let's get that fancy dinner I promised you," Luke said to Claire as they turned at the signpost that pointed the way to the food court.

"I'm not so sure a chili cheese dog is such a good idea after the cartwheels my insides have been turning today." Her eyes were scrunched with doubt.

He smiled and tugged on her hand to gain her cooperation. In the hours since her ordeal on the roller coaster she hadn't broken their contact for more than a couple of minutes. She'd clung to him as she climbed from the car, and held on while her wobbly legs returned to normal. Then she'd reached for his steadying support after each dizzying ride. The touch had turned to a comfortable connection that he couldn't help but enjoy.

The kids had snickered and pointed but soon seemed to ignore the hand-holding that was pretty commonplace stuff among the general population. But for Luke, the simple act was profound, and he was constantly aware of her warm touch. Her voluntary closeness could no longer be blamed on fear. He wanted to believe it was her wish to be near him, mostly because he was feeling the same. A need for this chaste contact gripped Luke.

"If your stomach's had all the adventure it can stand for one day I guess I can hunt you down a grilled chicken sandwich."

"You're too kind," she deadpanned. "But since you're to blame for my unstable insides, I'd say you at least owe me that much."

"Now wait a minute." He raised an eyebrow and cocked his head to the side. "After that ear-splitting scream I wouldn't have given a plug nickel for the chance of getting you on a second coaster, much less a third. *You're* the one who wanted to give it another shot."

"Guilty as charged." She ducked her head to hide her brief smile of accomplishment. "But it looked like fun and I didn't want to be left out again."

The wistful note in her voice told him she'd just shared something personal. He wanted to know more.

"Again? You've been here before?"

"Sure, but I've always been the responsible one who waited on the bench and held onto everybody's caps and purses."

"Even as a kid?" he asked, hearing the disbelief in his question.

She rolled her eyes. "Are you joking? At their age I didn't have time for amusement parks, and nobody would have invited me anyway. I was a private-school nerd who spent all my spare time involved in pageants. I didn't get asked out a single time in high school."

"Oh, please." He refused to accept that as fact. "A girl as beautiful as you didn't date?"

"My looks were just one more strike against me. The girls were jealous so they never included me, and the boys figured they wouldn't have a chance so they didn't bother asking."

Luke flashed back to a time when he never knew if he was liked for himself or for the fame and money he possessed. It only took a moment to connect with what she must have felt as a teenage girl who wasn't unconditionally accepted by her peers.

He stopped walking, stared down into her questioning eyes and squeezed her hand. "Well, this boy's gonna bother. Claire Savage, will you have dinner with me? A real dinner, not just fast food. We could drive down to the Kemah Boardwalk."

"Are you asking me on a *date?*" Her eyebrows shot up along with her voice.

"Well, no, but you don't have to sound so shocked by the possibility." His stomach knotted at the skepticism in her tone. Maybe he had been a bit hard on her. "Friends do occasionally spend time together, you know. We are friends, aren't we?" What a dweeb he was, asking for approval, not much better off than the junior high kids who'd pestered them all day.

She giggled behind her hand at his suggestion, sounding very young and innocent herself.

He pushed for an answer. "So, how's tomorrow night?"

"What about band practice?" The sparkle in her eyes said she wanted to agree but he'd already learned her nature was to think of others first.

"I'm gonna work those guys so hard tomorrow they'll need the night off to recover."

She stood on tiptoe and kissed his cheek. "Thanks for asking. Sure, I'll go to dinner with you…friend."

Before her heels touched the ground he pulled her to his chest and brought his lips down to meet hers.

Chapter Eight

Claire closed her eyes and gave in to the sweet moment. The kiss was unexpected and brief. Barely seconds elapsed and it was over. Luke ended the contact, and for the first time in her twenty-seven years Claire ached to continue.

This man was bringing so many new experiences into her life, most of them involving her emotions. And now, her heart was joining in the fun. The attraction was profound and profoundly confusing. They'd be headed down separate paths in a couple of weeks; Luke to the life on the road that he seemed to love and she to Sturgis and the excitement of the rally and the public unveiling of the Savage. What was God's purpose in bringing them together for this short time? Claire knew she was beginning to feel His healing touch through Luke, but would God send a man she could finally be comfortable with only to take him away?

As the canopy of dusk began to drape the park and streetlamps flickered to life, Claire searched Luke's rugged face for answers to her questions. Then she boldly spoke what was on her mind.

"Where is this headed, Luke?"

Still holding her in a loose embrace, he pressed his forehead to hers. She felt the warmth of his breath when he exhaled. He remained quiet as he seemed to consider the question, then finally spoke.

"Someplace I've never been before."

"Is that a good thing?"

"I guess that depends mostly on you, Claire. You don't seem to do anything without a lot of careful preparation, and I don't want my time here to throw a wrinkle in your plans."

She leaned her head back so she could see his face, but he kept his eyes closed. The opportunity was too perfect to resist. She turned her face to the side and rested her cheek against his chest. The rapid thumping of his heart was the confirmation she needed.

"You've ironed out more wrinkles in a few days than my therapist has in the past two years."

He kissed the top of her head and ended the hug but kept hold of her hand. "Someday we'll have to share our therapy stories, but right now let's eat." His lazy grin slid into place but a tender light she hadn't seen before glowed in his eyes.

* * *

Late the next morning, Luke enjoyed the solitude of his studio as he mulled over the strong emotions ignited by his time with Claire.

"Excuse me, Luke." Dana had slipped into the Praise Productions trailer so quietly he hadn't realized she was there. He swiveled his leather chair away from the mixing board to face her. Today she sported a dreadful Gothic getup, all black clothing and white makeup that gave her a seasick glow.

"What's up, lizard?"

They both smiled at the nickname he'd given her to acknowledge her quick-change, chameleon expression of fashion.

"I thought I should let somebody know that one of the girls is getting a little schizoid about Zach." Dana was overboard about the guys herself, but more like a protective sister than a crazed fan.

"Define schizoid."

She narrowed her kohl-rimmed eyes and pursed her maroon lips to telegraph gimme-a-break impatience.

"You know, getting all mental like some stalker. Zach gave Nicole Arnold a drumstick to shut her up and now she's saying nutso stuff about wanting to cut off one of his fingers so she can take a little piece of him home with her."

Luke grimaced at the image.

"Nice, huh?" Dana mirrored his reaction and nodded her head. "You want me to run her off?"

At the thought of tiny little Dana Stabler acting as bouncer for the Harvest Sons, he threw his head back and enjoyed the best laugh he'd had in weeks.

"You think I can't do it?" She took offense.

He wiped his eyes with the heels of both hands. "You, dear girl, can do anything you set your mind to. But don't you think there's a more Christian way to handle this?"

"Yeah, I guess so," she admitted.

Luke stood and lightly touched Dana's shoulder to guide her toward the door. "You've done your part. I'll take it from here."

Her clunky black boots tromped down the metal ramp he used to roll heavy equipment on and off the trailer. Luke spotted Pastor Ken's truck in its usual spot, closed and locked the door and headed toward the building.

He slipped into the back of the sanctuary and stood in the dim light to watch for a bit. The Sons were supposed to be running through the playlist Luke had arranged for them. They were ten days from recording and the dozen songs would have to be rehearsed hundreds of times.

Eric was seated on the apron of the stage, his long legs dangling. He was working on something with Brian, who seemed less surly and more at ease today. The brothers were beginning to believe in the potential of the group and their chance to get out from under the control of their volatile father. Eric was developing into a fine leader, mimicking Luke's coaching style, encouraging and probing, insisting on mastering the basics. He felt the flutter of what must have been a fatherly sense of pride.

"Thank You for leading me here," Luke whispered.

He glanced toward the back of the platform. Chad stood behind his electric keyboard, brows knit in concentration as he practiced the fingering of a tricky bridge. And Zach, the focus of a girl who wanted a hunk of his hand for a keepsake, practiced some fingering of his own as he twirled his drumsticks, tossing them high in the air for effect.

"Zach, work on your grooves and save the drum major routine for later," Luke barked as he trudged forward. Each boy snapped out of his personal fog and turned toward Luke's voice. He had their attention, might as well get some work done.

"Chad, let's hear that bridge from the top and lead straight into the last verse. Eric, the kids already know this song and they love it. Don't stress over your Spanish accent. Give it the emotion you do when you sing it in English and you'll have them at *hola*."

"*Muchas gracias, senor.*" Eric rolled his R's and grinned.

"Brian, I want to hear more bass in the closing

measures. You're exceptional on this number so bring it on, okay? *You* be the show-off brother for a change." He glared at Eric, who'd become almost overconfident in his stage presentation. Another similarity between Luke and this boy.

Brian ducked his head but nodded agreement. A little color rose in his pale cheeks indicating his pleasure. They picked up the number where Luke instructed. Downright impressed, he gave the Sons two thumbs up and motioned to continue as he left them to practice.

At midday the large lobby of the church was empty. He paused at the open door to Ken's study. Notes and candy wrappers spread across his desk, the pastor tapped away on his laptop.

"Am I interrupting?"

"Never," Ken answered without missing a keystroke. "Come on in, I'm at a good stopping place." He finished and snapped the lid down. "What's on your mind?"

"I'm in a situation I don't know how to handle and I could use some guidance and prayer," Luke said.

Had it really been less than a week since he'd sat in this room thinking he'd be the last person to make that admission? God did indeed work in strange ways, but Luke had accepted that long ago. He glanced up and down the hall to make sure no one was watching and then quietly closed the door.

* * *

As he drove, Luke surreptitiously examined his appearance and flipped the truck visor back into place. He hoped his visit to the barber wasn't an obvious sign of his last shred of vanity. It had been so long since he'd worried about his appearance and this silly concern was unsettling. After third degree burns had literally melted away his fame, he'd spent years avoiding mirrors. But there was no hiding from the look on the faces he'd encountered each day. His decision to undergo the painful and expensive reconstruction had been as much for the sake of others as for himself. He'd had a mission to fulfill and his appearance had become a distraction from the work he needed to accomplish. So he'd invested most of his savings in the surgeries and trusted God for the outcome.

Now he'd found a woman and a community that didn't seem to notice the last reminder of his foolish behavior. His heart told him to forget his past, but his instinct said otherwise. He had to remain vigilant. If the past caught up with him, the light of his mission would be snuffed out by the glare from his mistakes.

A huge billboard towering seventy-five feet above the interstate beckoned drivers toward the exit that would lead them to Savage Cycles of Houston. Luke parked his truck close to the building and wandered through the wide glass doors. He crossed the brick-colored floor and stood in the center of the showroom. Turning in a slow circle, he whistled appreciation for the "high priced toys" that Claire had mentioned.

He crossed to the display and openly admired the lead bike.

"Try it on," Claire called from across the room.

He turned to see her striding toward him, lovely as always. "You sure?" he asked.

"Of course. It's like buying a hat. You've got to find the one that fits you perfectly." She swept her hand in an arc, offering him a dozen to choose from.

"You don't have to tell me twice." He straddled the nearest one-of-a-kind Softail, settled against the plush leather and sighed his approval. "I bet the floors need mopping after men have been drooling over these bikes all day."

"We don't mind. It's a hazard of the business." She returned his quip. "Would you like that peek at my secret weapon now?"

"Absolutely," he agreed, glad she'd brought it up so he wouldn't have to ask again. Keeping the bike under wraps until the unveiling at the rally was probably an important part of her marketing strategy.

She led the way through the showroom to the private design shop in the back. On the wall was a full-scale black-ink rendering of the Savage. The incredible detail begged to be brought to life. As Luke stepped closer to admire the artist's work, Claire dimmed the overhead lights giving the illusion that the drawing was glowing from behind. The soft light source increased until there was no doubt that this canvas was actually a backlit screen.

At the touch of a button, the screen rose slowly on a hidden track revealing the Southern Savage showcased in a mirrored cave set back in the wall. Spotlights struck the super-stretch Softail from every angle. The beams served to deepen the hand-painted red-and-blue feathers floating on a field of white. The gas tank was detailed to resemble a head-dress fit for a Texas Comanche Chief.

"Whoa," Luke breathed, as he stepped into the private showcase and circled the bike.

"Isn't she incredible?"

He glanced up at Claire, who smiled her joy just as any proud parent might. He made several long strides to stand directly in front of the woman who had captured his attention.

"She's incredible all right," was his simple statement before his lips met hers.

Though still brief, the kiss was deeper than the one they'd shared the night before. Claire thanked God for Luke's tender and respectful approach. It was exactly what she needed but all she could handle.

"Amazing," he murmured.

"The Savage?"

"Yeah, the Claire Savage," he chuckled before stepping away. His gaze swept the design shop. "You've done an incredible job here and your bike is a masterpiece. I'm afraid we're about to lose you to the national media." He looked slightly sad, as if he truly meant the last statement.

She lowered the screen once again, removing the Savage from view. Then she slipped an arm through Luke's and escorted him through the showroom to the front counter where she'd left her bag and keys. "There's not much chance of that. You forget I've had some experience with the media. I know how to keep things under control."

Outside, he opened the truck door and held her hand as she stepped up into the cab. When she was seated he took both of her hands into his and seemed to study her eyes before he spoke.

"Claire, the press is vicious. They stalk you for money then leave your bloody body to the vultures. Don't think for a minute you can control them or that they're your friends. Trust me on this, okay?"

"Okay," she answered. He closed the door and rounded the back of the truck.

He was so intense, so sincere. There was more, she was sure of it but he'd have to share his secrets when he was ready. Just as she had to share hers with him.

* * *

"And this is Buck." Claire introduced the timid dachshund who shyly tucked his long nose beneath her arm to peek down at Luke.

"I think they like me," he observed from his spot on the floor. He'd squatted to make friends with Tripod and then settled into a cross-legged position so R.C. could curl his purring body comfortably into a friendly lap.

"Then it's unanimous." Claire kicked off her shoes and joined him on the Persian carpet with her back pressed against the navy leather sofa. With the three animals begging for attention, they felt chaperoned in her quiet townhome. "Thank you for dinner. The Flying Dutchman has always been one of my favorite restaurants but you didn't need to drive all the way to Kemah."

"When you live on the road you don't mind driving an hour out of the way for a good meal." He waved away any inconvenience.

"Where is home for you, Luke?" After their companionable meal she hoped he'd open up a bit.

"About six weeks a year it's a little place in south Georgia."

"Is that where your family is?"

"Not anymore. My old man was stationed at a nuclear sub base up the road in King's Bay. When he retired from the Navy in the late eighties they moved to Seattle and I stayed behind."

"You couldn't have been much more than a kid. That must have been a hard decision for your family."

He shook his head. "I'd been in boarding school all my life and we weren't seeing eye-to-eye on anything at the time, so nobody was too torn up about it."

Here was another clue into his very private side. Knowing the pain of a father who made no effort to be a part of her life, Claire was beginning to understand the gruff exterior Luke wore like armor to protect his heart.

"But you still see them, right?"

"Not since the summer after high school graduation. My father was so furious I thought he'd have a stroke when I chose music over the military."

"What about your mother? Didn't she support you?"

"My mother is nothing like yours, Claire. She's so caught up in the old man's career she'd do anything for him. She's happy playing Emma to his Admiral Lord Nelson."

"But they must be very proud of the work you do, Luke." She laid a hand gently on his forearm.

He stopped stroking the red tabby in his lap and raised serious eyes to stare at her.

"They have no idea where I am or what I do. We're all satisfied with the arrangement and that's final." His tone was firm, the matter was closed.

She put her hand back on Buck, who squirmed for attention. "How's it going with the Harvest Sons?" She changed the subject, hungry to know more about this man.

His eyes lit instantly when the topic shifted to his current project. "Those guys are awesome, Claire." He raised his eyebrows and nodded to emphasize his point. "Hands down they are the best group of young people I've worked with since I started Praise Productions."

"Have you told them that?"

"No way," he chuckled his response. "They're cocky enough without throwing kerosene on that fire. No, I want them to keep working as hard as they have this past week so this CD will be primo in every way. Then the next step will be to score a trustworthy manager who can take them professional."

R.C. stretched and purred as Luke began to scratch the cat's head. Tripod grumbled and stood to nudge Luke's shoulder. "These fellas are spoiled. You're going to have a hard time finding families to care for them the way you have."

"I was thinking the same thing about the Sons," she mused. "I can step in as a sponsor but there's nobody at Abundant Harvest who can fill your shoes. What do bands do after you're gone, Luke?"

An odd look of sadness flickered across his face.

"What is it?" she asked.

"I'm sorry to say I've never dwelt too much on

that in the past. When I meet my obligations and it's time to leave, I pack my stuff and move on. What the band or the church does after that is their business and that's by design." He stopped stroking the animals and leaned toward her.

"But this time I've given some thought to hanging around Houston a while longer. What do you think?"

Chapter Nine

Luke continued to stroke the soft tabby cat when what he really wanted was to run his hand through the many shades of Claire's silky blond hair. Her eyes had softened to the color of melted brown sugar when he'd mentioned staying longer and now the endearing smile on her soft lips told him she was pleased.

"Oh, Luke!" she squealed, sending all three animals scurrying. Instead of rushing to comfort her foster pets she twisted up onto her knees, laid her hands on either side of his face and planted an impetuous kiss directly on his mouth. "That would be wonderful," she breathed. "You know the Battle of the Bands is based in Houston and I bet you could find full-time employment with them."

"Wait—wait—wait a minute," he stammered. "I'm just thinking about staying a few weeks longer, not permanently."

The force of his words was water on a campfire, drowning her enthusiasm. As the moment of excitement slipped from her face, his gut twisted with remorse for giving voice to his thoughts. If it was painful just to talk about leaving, how much worse would it be when the time came?

"Claire, I love my work," he tried to explain. "God put me on this path as a mission and I don't know where He's leading me. Maybe this is my destination, I can't say right now. But I won't build expectations or make promises I can't keep. You know that about me already."

The muscles in her slender jaw flexed and she clenched her teeth as if holding back words that fought to be free. Her eyes telegraphed a mixture of sadness, anger, defiance and embarrassment—all signals that only served to puzzle him more.

He knew in his soul that her unconscious act of touching his face and kissing him had been a leap of faith on her part. Now his heart agonized because he couldn't make promises to her.

She began to pull away.

"No," he insisted. He placed his hands over hers and held her soft palms to his cheeks, a tender touch he hadn't known in many years. "Don't go. Kiss me again."

Where she'd been exuberant with confidence only moments before, now her eyes clouded with hesitation.

"Please," he whispered. "Kiss me again."

He lightened his hold on her hands, giving her control. Expecting she still might back away, he breathed a sigh of contentment when she slipped her hands around his neck and cupped his head. She dipped her face to his and took his mouth in a hesitant kiss.

Claire ended the moment with a giggle as Tripod poked them with his wiry muzzle, a jealous attempt to separate their embrace. Luke draped his arm over the edge of the sofa making a space for her to sit beside him.

"Don't give up on me." Their eyes locked and understandably, there was confusion in hers. "I mean it," he insisted. "Don't give up on me. I want whatever this is. But I made so many stupid mistakes early in my life, so now I try to take it slow and listen for God's voice. And He's telling me there are unsettled things in your life, too. I'm a pretty good listener if you wanna talk."

Claire's pride was still smarting from humiliation. The first overture she'd ever made to a man and it was almost a disaster. She wanted to laugh out loud at the irony. Claire Savage, the queen of preparation and timing, jumping the gun. Making a fool of herself once a day was enough, otherwise she might have risked telling him everything. He'd said he sensed something, said he was a good listener. But could he really understand the pain of wrestling an inner demon every day of his life?

Get 2 Books FREE!

Steeple Hill Books,
publisher of inspirational romance fiction, presents

Love Inspired

A series of contemporary love stories that will lift your spirits and reinforce important lessons about life, faith and love!

FREE BOOKS!
Get two free books by best-selling, inspirational authors!

FREE GIFT!
Get an exciting surprise gift absolutely free!

2 FREE BOOKS

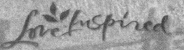

Love Inspired

▲ To get your 2 free books and a free gift, affix this peel-off sticker to the reply card and mail it today!

Get 2

HOW TO GET YOUR
2 FREE BOOKS AND FREE GIFT

1. Peel off the 2 FREE BOOKS sticker from the front cover. Place it in the space provided at right. This automatically entitles you to receive two free books and an exciting surprise gift.

2. Send back this card and you'll get 2 Love Inspired® books. These books have a combined cover price of $9.98 in the U.S. and $11.98 in Canada, but they are yours to keep absolutely FREE!

3. There's <u>no</u> catch. You're under <u>no</u> obligation to buy anything. We charge nothing – ZERO – for your first shipment. And you don't have to make any minimum number of purchases – not even one!

4. We call this line Love Inspired because each month you'll receive books that are filled with joy, faith and traditional values. The stories will lift your spirits and gladden your heart! You'll like the convenience of getting them delivered to your home well before they are in stores. And you'll love our discount prices, too!

5. We hope that after receiving your free books you'll want to remain a subscriber. But the choice is yours – to continue or cancel, anytime at all! So why not take us up on our invitation, with no risk of any kind. You'll be glad you did!

6. And remember…we'll send you a surprise gift ABSOLUTELY FREE just for giving Love Inspired novels a try!

Steeple Hill®

® and TM are trademarks owned and used by the trademark owner and/or its licensee.

SPECIAL FREE GIFT!!

We'll send you a fabulous surprise gift, absolutely FREE, simply for accepting our no-risk offer!

Order online at:
www.LoveInspiredBooks.com

©1997 STEEPLE HILL BOOKS

Books FREE!

DETACH AND MAIL CARD TODAY!

HURRY!
Return this card promptly to get
2 FREE books
and a FREE gift!

Love Inspired®

YES, please send me the 2 FREE *Love Inspired* books and FREE gift for which I qualify. I understand that I am under no obligation to purchase anything further, as explained on the opposite page.

affix
free
books
sticker
here

313 IDL EE4E   113 IDL EE4Q

FIRST NAME   LAST NAME

ADDRESS

APT.#   CITY

STATE/PROV   ZIP/POSTAL CODE

(LI-LA-06)

Steeple Hill Reader Service™—Here's How It Works:

Accepting your 2 free books and gift places you under no obligation to buy anything. You may keep the books and gift and return the shipping statement marked "cancel." If you do not cancel, about a month later we will send you 4 additional books and bill you just $3.99 each in the U.S., or $4.74 each in Canada, plus 25¢ shipping & handling per book and applicable taxes if any.* That's the complete price, and — compared to cover prices of $4.99 each in the U.S. and $5.99 each in Canada — it's quite a bargain! You may cancel at any time, but if you choose to continue, every month we'll send you 4 more books, which you may either purchase at the discount price...or return to us and cancel your subscription.

*Terms and prices subject to change without notice. Sales tax applicable in N.Y.
Canadian residents will be charged applicable provincial taxes and GST.

If offer card is missing write to: Steeple Hill Reader Service, 3010 Walden Ave., P.O. Box 1867, Buffalo, NY 14240-1867

BUSINESS REPLY MAIL

FIRST-CLASS MAIL   PERMIT NO. 717-003   BUFFALO, NY

POSTAGE WILL BE PAID BY ADDRESSEE

STEEPLE HILL READER SERVICE
3010 WALDEN AVE
PO BOX 1867
BUFFALO NY 14240-9952

NO POSTAGE
NECESSARY
IF MAILED
IN THE
UNITED STATES

She exhaled a deep breath and began. But instead of exposing her painful childhood, she poured her concerns out about her decision to switch careers, going toe-to-toe with the established dealers in a decidedly male-dominated industry. In response to his thoughtful questions, she even disclosed the nature of her financial risk. She studied the books every day and knew her worth as well as her debt to the last penny. The building was mortgaged to the skies but there was plenty of equity in the business to expand down the road.

So much of her future hinged on the success of the dealership and the Southern Savage in particular. She'd taken a calculated gamble knowing the odds were against her. But she'd been on the losing side of life before and she was still standing. If worse came to worse, with God's help she'd survive again.

After Luke had gone, she sat on the leather sofa surrounded by her pets, breathing in the manly scent that lingered. She examined her heart over and over and there was no denying it. Luke Dawson was getting under her skin. She'd touched his face and kissed him, more than once. He'd asked her not to give up on him. They'd shared some details of their dreams. But he couldn't promise he'd stay.

"Father God," she prayed aloud. "If it's Your perfect will for our lives, please show me that Luke's a

man I can trust with my heart. And if he is I promise I won't make the same mistake Mama did and
let him leave without a fight."

A small fear had nagged Luke for days. What
right did he have to ask a beauty like Claire Savage
to wait on a man like him while he stumbled through
his maze of feelings? She had life by the tail and any
man would be a fool to expect her to sit patiently for
very long. Since the morning he'd signed the papers
to officially incorporate Praise Productions, there
had never been a doubt that his life's purpose was
to be on the road, working with young people, doing
what he could to give them the right start.

But two nights ago, Claire's mention of a possible association with Houston's Battle of the Bands
had begun to stir an idea he might never have
considered on his own. Now, like Freeway with a
forbidden leather shoe, Luke quietly chewed on the
idea that had filled a dozen pages in his notebook.
The kids would come to him. He could audition
them during the weeks of the competition and then
work up his recording schedule a year at a time. If
he found the right local studio to partner with he
should be able to make ends meet and still keep his
rates low.

And he'd be with Claire.

Luke paused from the chore of rolling cabinets
filled with equipment across the parking lot from the

trailer to the sanctuary. The recording date was a little more than a week away. Tonight was a practice run-through and he had plenty of time left to set up for the drill.

He leaned an elbow atop a stack of amps and rested his chin on his hand as he studied the skyline in the distance. In the few hours he and Claire had shared since their evening alone, they'd constantly been surrounded by their Abundant Harvest family. He was anxious for more. Simply being near her wasn't enough. He wanted to explore a future with her.

"Lemme give you a hand with that," Zach called as he loped across the parking lot.

"Knock yourself out," Luke agreed, and let Zach do the pushing as they headed for the side entrance. "Why aren't you at work?"

"The lunch crowd was light today so they let me off. Thought I'd get in some practice while the church is empty."

"Good idea. I know it gets crazy with so many people around."

"Speaking of crazy, Dana told me she talked to you about that nut case, Nicole."

Luke scowled at the thoughtless comment, but knew it was exactly what he'd have said at that age. "Yes, she did, and I went straight to Pastor Ken."

Zach scowled and squeezed his eyes shut. "Aww, man! Why'd you do that?"

"Because if you're a responsible adult working on church property, that's what you're expected to do when a young person could be in trouble."

"I'm not in trouble," Zach insisted.

"But Nicole could be. A girl who makes comments about lopping off somebody's finger for a keepsake is definitely in need of attention."

"Oh, just ignore her. If she shows up again I'll handle it."

"How?" Luke pressed.

"I'll tell her to get lost. I'm tired of having her around anyway."

Luke grabbed the handle of the amp case, yanked it free from Zach's grasp and pushed it himself.

"Hey! Why'd you do that?" Zach stopped to stare at Luke.

"Because I'm too busy to put up with you today." Luke turned his back on the boy and continued to muscle the heavy equipment across the asphalt.

"But it's my turn. That's why I'm here early," Zach admitted, his voice rising an octave from the sting of Luke's words. "Luke?" Zach took three quick steps and grabbed his mentor by the arm.

Luke shook off the boy's grasp and ignored the gleam of rejection in his eyes. "Do I need to talk slower so you can understand, Zach? I'm sick of you constantly being under my feet, so get lost." He continued toward the building, not looking back. When he reached the security door he punched in the pass code and pulled it wide. After he'd maneuvered the cabinet through the opening he turned toward the spot where Zach still waited. His arms hung limp at his sides and his shoulders slumped. He stared at his feet and for once his shaggy head wasn't tilted back with pride.

"So," Luke raised his voice. "How does it feel?"

"Huh?" Zach's head popped up.

"That's what you planned to tell Nicole, right? So how does it feel to be blown off by somebody you like?"

"Oh, I get it." Zach's smile was back in place as he hurried to catch up. "You were just scammin' me."

"Wrong answer, dude. Now think back thirty seconds if you can remember that far and tell me how you felt."

"Like pond scum."

"Good." Luke nodded, glad to know he'd gotten through to Zach. "Jesus said 'What you do to the least of these you do to me.' So try to remember that, too, before you make somebody feel like they're not wanted."

"So, what am I supposed to do if Nicole shows up again tonight?"

"Be kind to her and if she forces the issue tell her very respectfully that you're not interested. And leave the rest to me and Claire."

A sly smile curved Zach's lips. "You wouldn't be a little sweet on Miss Claire, would ya?"

"Mind your own business," Luke snapped.

Zach laughed. "Yeah, we're on to you two." He continued to press his luck even though Luke slipped into his practiced angry glare. "Hey, it's cool. Miss Claire's a babe. Go for it, man."

Luke gave the boy a lighthearted shove into the building and pulled the door shut behind them.

Claire clapped in time with the drumbeat, amazed along with everyone else that over the past week the Harvest Sons had completely transformed their style. Luke's skills for coaching and musical arrangement were evident in the band's new sound. Their self-confidence had blossomed thanks to the encouragement and guidance that had been added to their lives since the arrival of Luke Dawson.

His grouchy act was slipping. The tender heart of a Christian man beat beneath that ever-present black T-shirt. He cared about the Sons, the Abundant Harvest community and, Claire believed, he cared about her, too.

More importantly, the kisses she'd initiated had been glimpses of the breakthrough she'd prayed for. Finally, the closeness of a man didn't repulse her or intensify her dark dreams.

Nicole Arnold tugged at the shirt that was two sizes too small to cover her abdomen. The girl's low-slung jeans were indecently tight, especially for a church activity. But there were few restrictions on the youth that would discourage participation. Word was out that the Sons were producing a CD, so the Friday night practice was packed with high schoolers who'd normally be at the mall or movie theater. Another testimony to the power of contemporary Christian music.

The set ended, the lights came up and the guys held court in front of the stage, enjoying the attention and well-deserved praise. Claire watched the control booth for some sign of Luke. Her chest tingled with an unfamiliar flutter that she could only presume came from being attracted to a man. She experienced a breathless sensation each time she remembered his mossy green eyes or handsome smile.

The red "recording" light went dark, signaling that he'd be out shortly. She edged through the crowd of youngsters, stopping when she reached the spot where Nicole chewed her fingernail and waited for her turn to congratulate Zach.

"Weren't they great?" Claire spoke casually to the girl.

"Oh, hi, Miss Claire." Nicole barely took her eyes off her idol long enough to acknowledge the greeting. "Yes, Zach was awesome."

"I'm glad to see you back tonight because I wanted to ask you for some help."

Nicole turned surprised gray eyes to Claire. "Me?" She continued nibbling her nail.

"Sure." Claire laughed at the girl's disbelief. "We're looking for some summer help down at Savage Cycles and you've been around here so much lately I thought you might have time for a job. You interested?"

The young face brightened with enthusiasm and her hand fell to her side as she abandoned the nervous habit. Claire was reminded of pageant contestants who bit their nails bloody all week long and then applied acrylic to hide the telling damage on stage. She was grateful that Luke had included her in this plan to find Nicole a positive interest to occupy her mind.

"Wow, yes!" She jumped at the offer. Then a frown of worry crossed her face. "I'm kinda broke right now. Would I have to have new clothes for work?" she asked, tugging at her top again.

"Don't worry, your jeans are fine and we've got some great T-shirts. We'll give you several in the right size to wear for work." Claire draped her arm around the girl's shoulders and gave her a side squeeze. "You'll fit right in."

The gratitude in Nicole's eyes lodged a lump in Claire's throat. Helping this teen overcome her awkward fears and the intense need to belong was better than a month of therapy. For both of them.

"Be there at seven tomorrow morning, and ask for

Justin. He'll need an hour to get you organized before we start inventory at eight."

"No problem." She beamed at the prospect of employment.

Luke appeared in the aisle, gave a wrap-it-up hand signal to the band and then winked at Claire. Though she was still busy distracting Nicole, focusing on their conversation was almost impossible with her pulse tap dancing over Luke's small overture.

"I brought Chinese food for the band," Claire continued. "Would you like to join us?"

Nicole checked the time on the cell phone clipped to her waistband. "No thanks. I better catch a ride home if I have to start work in the morning. My dad's gonna freak," she said with pride. She dug into her oversize shoulder bag, pulled out a drumstick and handed it to Claire. "Would you give this back to Zach for me and tell him I had to take off?"

"Sure thing."

The two exchanged another quick hug and the girl joined a throng of kids who headed for the parking lot.

"How'd it go?" Luke was close at her side, smiling down.

"Almost too easy." She waggled the drumstick between her thumb and forefinger. "We didn't even need to get into phase two of our plan. She was so glad to have a job that she asked me to give this back to Zach so she could hurry home to tell her dad. She seemed to think he'd be pleased."

"Thanks," Luke said. The intense color of his eyes softened as he spoke, his gaze a caress on her face. "Did you really need help at work? I can give you the money to pay her."

Claire waved away his offer.

"Actually, we do. I have all the guys working double duty to get ready for Sturgis. We'll keep her so busy she won't have time to obsess over Zach."

Luke couldn't hold back any longer. He boldly lifted his hand and brushed the long bangs to the side so he could experience the unforgettable power of her eyes. After his prayers at night, the gleaming hot caramel of Claire's eyes occupied his mind as he fell asleep. His gaze locked on hers and his chest ached exquisitely with the need to express the new feelings spilling from his heart. If anybody was obsessing, it was him.

And if it hadn't been completely inappropriate, he'd have kissed her right then and there.

Chapter Ten

The mouth-watering aromas from almond chicken and sweet-and-sour pork wafted over the scarred table in the fellowship hall where they shared nightly meals.

"Oh, Luke!" Her eyes widened as she remembered something important. She dropped her chopsticks and wiped her fingers on a paper napkin. "I was so preoccupied with the Nicole thing I forgot to show you this."

The energy of Claire's voice was becoming more addictive than his morning coffee. He craved hearing her Texas accent, sharing her childlike thrill over every accomplishment, hers or anybody else's. He watched as she flipped open her folder of sheet music and pulled out several pages that she proudly extended.

"Art said the issue hits the newsstands tomorrow."

"Art said," Luke mimicked, knowing he deserved the punch she landed against his shoulder.

With the launch of The Southern Savage at the Sturgis Bike Rally, Claire Savage puts the industry on notice. This former Miss Texas is about to invade the custom chopper market.

Luke silently read the text. Seeing her name on the faxed pages quickened the blood flow in his veins. His excitement for her was dampened by the memory of how easily the press could turn. One day you were their darling. The next they were hounds after your scent. If she truly wanted national attention, this was her ticket to the show. For her sake he'd try to ignore the familiar foreboding that hunkered in silence at the edge of his emotions.

"What do you think?" There was such hope in her voice.

"Great piece." He told her what she needed to hear. "That American-only business is really gonna get attention. Better budget some of your time for all the follow-up work this is bound to generate." He handed over the pages.

Her eyebrows drew together and the edges of her mouth curved downward. "I hadn't planned on that. There aren't enough hours in the day to get everything done as it is."

He returned her chopsticks to her hand. "Eat."

She scooped up shrimp fried rice as he continued. "You'll need your strength 'cause this is no time to slack off. If local media shows up, talk to them. If the phone rings, handle the calls. You never know what form opportunity may take. You told me yourself what's at stake. Don't let anything stand between you and your dream. Leave this place to me and go take care of business."

Her enticing eyes narrowed. "Are you trying to get rid of me?"

"That never crossed my mind." He leaned closer. "But they do say absence makes the heart grow fonder."

The creases of humor at the corners of her eyes softened at his mention of fondness. He knew it was so much more than that but wouldn't rush to put words to the feelings that were costing him concentration and sleep.

"Will you call me after rehearsal tomorrow night to tell me what I missed?"

"You know how late it'll be." He knew he shouldn't start the high school ritual of the midnight phone call.

"I don't mind." She stabbed a mushroom with the tip of her chopstick and brandished it to emphasize her point. "In fact, I'll be angry with you if you don't tell me *everything*. Promise?"

"I promise," he said, knowing he was becoming a fool for her playful insistence.

* * *

At ten the next morning Luke took a break from the mixing board to investigate voices outside his trailer door. The fish-eye peep hole revealed Pastor Ken standing next to Moe Sanders, the elderly church administrator and self-appointed morality police chief. Ken said the search committee was interviewing for Moe's replacement so he could retire. In Luke's opinion, they needed to hurry. As Sanders raised his knuckles to wrap on the surface, Luke startled the fussbudget by swinging the door wide.

"Dawson, step outside," Sanders demanded. "We need a word with you," he insisted, his voice ringing with superiority as he waited for Luke to comply.

Luke ignored the always grumpy little man, took three steps down to the ground and fixed his gaze on the pastor. "What's up, Ken?"

"I'll tell you what's up—"

"Let me handle this, Moe." Ken's raised eyebrows and widened eyes were a silent apology.

"There's a Detective Garrison here. He's from the fraud division of the state attorney general's office. He's come to question you about complaints."

"Complaints?" Luke was incredulous. He'd never even had an issue that lead to a refund, let alone an investigation of fraud.

Ken nodded. "I think you'd better come talk to the man for yourself."

"I concur with the pastor. Follow me," Sanders instructed, pompously taking the lead as if the other two couldn't find the way on their own.

"Sorry about this, Luke."

"Hey, don't apologize. Let's get to the bottom of this so we can go back to work."

An unfamiliar, fortysomething man in a suit and tie stood as Luke entered the pastor's study. "Detective Phil Garrison." He flipped open a black leather wallet exposing a badge, then dropped it into his breast pocket and extended his hand. "I'm with the Texas state attorney general's office."

"Luke Dawson, Praise Productions," Luke introduced himself as they shook hands.

"You're welcome to talk in here." Ken motioned toward his small conference table.

"Please stay, Pastor," Luke invited. "I have nothing to hide from you." The three men moved toward the table.

Sanders, still standing in the doorway, leaned his head back, pursed fleshy lips and looked down his narrow nose at the others.

"You, too, Moe." Luke included the nosy old guy who would listen at the door otherwise. Might as well let him get the facts firsthand. Sanders sniffed and checked his watch, as if he had better things to do, then took the chair at the head of the table that was generally reserved for the pastor.

"Mr. Dawson, I'm here in cooperation with the

California Attorney General. Are you familiar with an outfit in Los Angeles doing business as Rambling Records?"

"I am." Luke nodded. "They're on the list of duplication houses that I provide for my clients."

"When was the last time you worked with Scott Rambling?"

"I've never worked with him myself. Rambling is not directly connected with Praise Productions."

"But you get a kickback on every job you refer, correct?"

"Absolutely not," Luke snapped and pushed away from the table. "And I don't appreciate the insinuation."

Sanders smacked his lips and leaned forward, eager for the details.

"Just doing my job, sir. No need to get excited."

Luke stood. "You imply that the integrity of my reputation is in question and then tell me not to get excited. Look, Garrison, either be specific about what's going on or instruct me to call a lawyer."

"This is only a fact-finding conversation to see if the charges being made against Rambling Records merit a full investigation. So a lawyer won't be necessary. Not yet, anyway."

"Detective, can you share any details of the charges?" Ken asked, obviously sensing the heat Luke felt rising in his neck.

Garrison pulled a small notepad from his breast

pocket and consulted the pages. "It seems Mr. Dawson here worked with several congregations who contracted with Rambling to mass produce their CDs. Scott Rambling appears to be quite a salesman. He not only filled their orders, he talked them out of investment capital to expand his business. Then he filed for bankruptcy and left the state. When the churches contacted the attorney general's office to make complaints, their questioning turned up your name, Mr. Dawson. You seem to be the common denominator."

Luke sent up a silent prayer for self-control as he gripped the edge of the table, imagining it was Scott Rambling's neck. The man had ripped off those congregations just as surely as if he'd stolen the money right out of the collection plate. And now Luke looked like an accomplice.

Ken rose and went to his desk. He pulled some pages from a stack of paperwork and carried them along with his candy dish back to the table. After flipping to the last page he handed the papers to Garrison. "This is the list Luke provided as part of his services. There are eight companies there and one of them happens to be Rambling Records." He handed Luke a candy bar and then unwrapped one for himself. "How many jobs did you work in California last year, Luke?"

"Ten."

"Ten," Ken repeated for Garrison's benefit before

popping the chocolate into his mouth. "And only three have contacted the attorney general." Ken narrowed his eyes while he chewed, as if thinking through the equation. "That tells me this is a random selection process from a short list and those three churches just happened to make the same choice. Wouldn't you agree that's a possibility, Detective?"

Garrison stared at the candy dish. "Oh, excuse my poor manners," Ken apologized, and handed the other two men chocolate bars.

"It's a possibility, sure," Garrison answered. "But the folks in those congregations lost a bunch of money and they're not going to drop this because I take them a *possible* answer. So until we reach a conclusion that satisfies the complainants and the fraud division I'll be asking a lot more questions."

Luke stood. "When you want to talk again, give me twenty-four hours notice so I can arrange to have an attorney present. Otherwise, I have seven days to do about two weeks worth of work so the Harvest Sons can record next Saturday."

Garrison closed his notebook and slipped it into his pocket. He handed business cards to all three men. "Mr. Dawson, please let me know where you can be reached in case you move on before our investigation is complete. You're not an easy man to track down."

Luke caught the look that passed from Moe Sanders to the pastor. How long would it take for the senior church administrator to turn Ken Allen against a virtual stranger who had been "tracked down" by a state investigator?

Sunday mornings were normally a time of peace and reflection for Claire, but today she was a tightly stretched rubber band, waiting to snap. Sitting behind the wheel of her pony car she drummed the fingers of her right hand on the gearshift knob and wiggled her foot to an imaginary cadence. She slapped the visor down and flipped open the vanity mirror. Thanks goodness her mother was thousands of miles away on that cruise ship otherwise she'd be amazed by her daughter's lack of grooming.

Claire's lip gloss had been gnawed off, her hair was blown every which way, her skin was threatening to break out and she was actually sweating. She was a mess.

And her exterior was composed compared to the hornet's nest of trouble that threatened her insides. The message on her home voicemail, calling a crisis meeting of the finance committee over the Praise Production contract, had thrown her into a near panic. She'd approved the contract and Moe Sanders wanted her opinion on some potential legal problem with Luke. It was no secret the old-fashioned administrator was against funding the Harvest Sons recording a CD from the start and now it seemed he had cause to interfere with the plan. The production was six days away. If word reached the boys before the facts were straight they'd be devastated.

This was her payback for taking the day off and fielding reactions to the *Today's Times* article. After twenty-four hours away from her church family, focusing on nothing but her personal business, she was worn down and out of touch. Maybe the publicity hadn't been such a blessing after all.

As Luke had predicted, the magazine was still warm on the stands when the phone started ringing. She'd talked to more potential customers in ten hours then she had in ten weeks. But for every customer call, there were two from the press. She'd even had a radio talk show try to put her on the air. By five she'd forwarded her phone to voice mail. Her gut told her that any free time should be spent with Luke.

Now she knew why.

He'd promised to call her last night. *He'd promised.* Luke didn't break promises. Something was terribly wrong and she needed to hear about it directly from him.

He refused to carry a cell phone but he'd given her the address of the weekly rental apartments where he was registered. She sat by the curb, searching the resident's parking lot for his truck. At ten minutes after seven his big diesel rumbled past the leasing office and slowed as he pulled up beside her. His window slid down and Luke lifted a paper cup in salute as Freeway woofed a greeting from the passenger's seat.

"Why didn't you call me?" she demanded.

"And good morning to you, too, Miss Texas," he responded. His voice lacked the usual wise-guy tone. His eyes were hidden behind dark glasses and his easy smile was missing.

"I've been worried sick about you, Luke."

"I'm sorry, sugar. It was a long night. Let's go talk." He tilted his head, indicating she should follow him, and pulled away.

She sat motionless, suspended between anger and elation. The fingers that had been drumming now shook with nervous excitement. The fear that something was out of kilter was replaced by hope that everything would be all right.

He'd called her sugar. She hadn't been the object of that endearment since the last time her father had phoned, two years ago.

Accompanying Luke across the threshold of his modest rental was like stepping back in time for Claire. The days of secondhand school clothes and cheap garage sale furniture loomed in her memory, a patchwork quilt of desperate times and simple comforts. Unable to manage the mortgage on her own, Claire's mother had sold their home and moved the two of them into a small apartment where every dime made a difference. Claire got her big dreams from her father, but Mary Savage cobbled the ideas into a plan that became reality. Certain there were plenty of times her mother had done without necessities so there would be money in the tight budget for entry fees, costumes and lessons, Claire was determined to give back to the woman who'd never filed for divorce and still prayed that one day her husband would come home.

Freeway took a sniffing tour of the small rooms, then plopped his belly on the kitchen's scarred linoleum floor. Luke turned off the countertop television and pulled out a ladder-backed dinette chair for Claire. He dropped his dark glasses on the tabletop and slumped into a chair angled to face her.

"You're gonna be late for the early service."

"Does it look like I'm dressed for church?" She held her arms out to the side and cocked her head while he looked her up and down. She'd stepped into dollar store flip-flops, baggy jeans and a wrinkled cotton shirt that had cooled in the bottom of the dryer.

"Now that you mention it, you are lookin' more like the rest of us today," he observed.

She wouldn't normally have picked up the newspaper at the end of the driveway in such an unkempt state, but she was in a hurry to get out of the house and the clothes were handy. He, of course, was already in his standard attire but his usual air of unquestioned control was missing. The dark blur beneath his eyes testified to her suspicion that he hadn't slept.

"Moe Sanders called an emergency meeting of the committee that approved your contract. He said you're being investigated for fraud."

The muscles in Luke's jaw tensed at the accusation.

"What's this all about, Luke? And why didn't you call last night and tell me about it yourself?"

"It was so late when we wrapped and I had a lot of praying and thinking to do."

She leaned forward and rested the back of her hand on his knee, palm open. The offer of her hand was the closest thing she'd ever made to an offer of her heart. She prayed he would accept both.

He scooped her cool fingers between his warm palms and as the heat from his body flowed into hers, she felt the skittering of his nervous pulse.

Luke. Rock-steady, in-charge Luke was worried sick.

Or was there more? Was he guilty?

Her chest ached with the thought that this man could possibly be dishonest, could have played them all for fools.

"Tell me what happened," she encouraged him, as all other thoughts vanished like vapor in the wind.

"Evidently, one of the duplication houses where I've been referring work went belly up, but only after the owner smooth-talked three of my client churches out of major investment capital. The obvious conclusion of the California State Attorney

General's office is that I must be part of the scam."
His voice was near to breaking with indignation as
he relayed the details of yesterday's meeting with
Detective Garrison.

Her world quaked at the accusation. If she'd been
the financial consultant for those churches, she would
have considered the circumstances and might possibly have come to the same deduction. So rather than
spin mental arguments for Luke's guilt or innocence,
she needed hard evidence. And so did Abundant
Harvest.

She let go of Luke's hand and grabbed her purse.
Puffing a breath upward she got the bangs off her
lashes so she could search the dark contents of the
leather bag for her address book.

"Luke, do you mind if I get Daniel Stabler involved?"

"Dana's father?"

"He's a Texas Ranger."

"I don't think so." Luke shook his head.

Her gaze darted from her purse to Luke. Did he
have something to hide?

"Daniel is one of the most acclaimed investigative officers in the country. Let's see what he can find
on Rambling Records."

Luke closed his eyes, ducked his chin and rubbed
both palms across the close-cropped hair on his
scalp. His fingers groped his skull like he was digging for answers. A deep sigh escaped his chest and

with the breath Claire heard something akin to despair.

"I don't want to blow this into something big. I'd just as soon pay back the losses myself than have my personal business put under a microscope."

"Just let me give it one shot. We'll keep it simple," she promised.

He nodded, seemed resigned.

In his place would she feel the same? Personal business had the right to remain private, but if there was nothing to hide...

She forced her eyes away from the man she cared about more than good sense dictated and glanced around his meager accommodations. There was nothing of value here. His financial worth seemed to be tied up in his truck and recording trailer. Where would he get the funds to even consider restitution as an option?

As much as she wanted to stay with Luke she needed to head home. She had two calls to make before she showered and dressed for church. Two people to reach out to on this disturbing Sunday morning.

A Texas Ranger and an investment broker.

Chapter Eleven

After he left the last worship service, Luke sought out the small meeting room that was crowded with members of the finance committee and church council. Only a few chairs in the front remained so he found a spot in the back, leaned one shoulder against the wall and fought down the sense that he was about to be prosecuted by a kangaroo court. Flashes of similar events throughout his life had been on constant replay in his mind for the past twenty-four hours. It was always the same. Just about the time he believed he could depend on somebody, they yanked the rug out from under him. Sadly, it seemed this place would be no different.

Heads turned to identify the latecomer. Hands lifted in greeting but smiles were weak. He couldn't blame them. He was a virtual stranger spending lots of hours with some of their kids. Now there was an accusation that he might be involved in bilking congregations out of tens of thousands of dollars. Scott Rambling must have been quite the smooth talker to convince the otherwise cautious conservatives to take such a risk. Luke stared at the toes of his sneakers and waited, certain he knew what was coming.

Ken Allen passed through the doorway followed by Claire and a tall, lean man in his early forties. He wore cowboy boots and carried a summer-weight, western straw hat in his large hands. The two men made their way through the rows of folding chairs, but Claire slipped across the back of the room, stopped on the far side of Luke, and then rested her hand lightly on his shoulder blade. The hidden contact went unnoticed by everyone except Luke, and to him it was a touch that sent a shockwave of reality through his body.

He turned his head slightly, and mouthed "Thank you." She responded with a reassuring pat on his back, the warm hand of the woman he loved resting gently against his skin.

Yes, the woman he *loved*.

"Let's get through this so we can all go home to Sunday dinner." Ken rubbed his flat stomach and the council snickered at their pastor's effort to lighten the moment.

"For the past week, that man back there—" Ken gestured toward Luke and heads turned in acknowledgement "—has been giving Abundant Harvest about eighteen hours of his time a day. Our boys have shown more improvement after a few days of his coaching than they did during all the months they prepared for the Battle of the Bands. On top of that, Luke has involved several more of our kids in this project who might otherwise be at home alone all summer. Instead of getting into who knows what, they're helping out at the church, learning to run our A/V equipment. And, as if that's not enough, he chaperoned our middle schoolers' day trip this past week. You parents of teens know that's above and beyond a volunteer job. We should be offering hazard pay to Luke on top of his contract rates." Ken laughed along with the rest and then continued.

"Luke hasn't asked for one cent up front of the incredible deal he gave us, he's guaranteed his work for a year, and he's left it up to us to decide who we'll do business with once it's time to reproduce the master recording. Now, I don't know about the rest of you, but everything I've seen of this man says he has a heart for the Lord and for our kids."

Years ago, there was a time when such personal accolades meant little to Luke. When he was young and invincible he'd believed his own press. Expected to be told how great he was. Today he knew better, and the supportive words of this man of God meant more to Luke than any music award in the business.

Ken continued, "The Harvest Sons have a recording session scheduled for next weekend and I, for one, am going to give Luke all the help he needs to prepare our boys for their professional debut." A loud exhale punctuated his speech. "Now, does anybody else have something they want to say?"

"I do, Pastor," Moe Sanders announced as he stood and edged his way through the chairs to the front of the room. "I think we need to nip this thing in the bud before our kids get hurt. Chances are Mr. Dawson's on the up and up but if it turns out he's not, then anybody associated with him will be dragged into the dirt. I say we pay him for the work he's done so far and then hire somebody local to finish what Dawson started. It's the safe thing to do."

"And since when are we called as Christians to do the *safe* thing?"

Luke's head snapped to the left as others turned in their chairs toward Claire's voice. Her hand slid from its hiding place on his back to grasp him by the forearm, a physical show of approval.

"Please, somebody remind me of the scripture where Jesus suggested we stay away from unsafe situations?" She shook her head, indicating such a passage didn't exist. "I'm pretty sure that when He ate with sinners or healed lepers He wasn't too concerned about whether or not it was safe."

"Young lady, you know that's not what I meant," Moe sputtered.

"But it's the same thing whether that's what you intended or not. Life is about taking risks, and as

Christians we're called to put ourselves out there for the sake of the gospel of Christ. That's what Luke is all about. What he does is not just his job, it's his mission. I've been watching him with the kids night after night and he's not only teaching them about the music business, he's planting seeds of faith in kids who may not get the message any other way." She squeezed Luke's arm as her warm gaze seemed to search his face for confirmation of what she'd said before turning back to the packed room.

"Come and see for yourselves this evening. He'll be here with your kids for hours after you're already home in bed. Stick around and volunteer for a while if you don't believe me."

"Claire's right," the tall cowboy spoke up.

"Y'all know Daniel Stabler." Ken made the introduction.

Standing in the front of the room next to Ken, the man was at ease with his Stetson in his hands.

"Since Mr. Dawson invited my Dana to be part of his recording team, she's really come out of her shell."

"Which shell would that be, Dan?" a man in the back called.

They laughed agreeably over the young girl's well-known propensity for costume changes.

"Whichever one she was hidin' in at the time."

Gripping the brim of his hat, he bumped it lightly against the outside of his leg and shrugged broad shoulders beneath his starched white dress shirt.

"That child has always been a puzzle to me, but the past week it's like she's found her purpose and she's finally feelin' good about who she is and what she's gonna do with her life." He chuckled, a rueful sound. "Of course, bein' a female she's entitled to change her mind a few more times, and bein' my Ladybug that includes her clothes, too."

Stabler made his way to the back of the room stood before Luke. "I wanna shake the hand of the gentleman who's helped my baby girl and I'd also like to extend my services to Mr. Dawson in any way he might need them to settle this mess out in California."

"Please call me Luke." The two men shook. "I appreciate your offer of help but it really won't be necessary."

"Well, I'm here for you if you need me," Stabler insisted. "For anything at all."

Luke was struck once again by the generosity of spirit of most of the folks in this suburban community of Houston.

"Luke, is there anything you want to say?" Ken motioned for Luke to take the floor.

"No thanks, Pastor Ken. I've always let my work speak for itself. If you folks decide you'd rather not have me stick around, there won't be any hard feelings."

"Then will you excuse us for some private discussion?"

Luke nodded agreement and prepared to turn toward the door. Claire's grip on his left arm held him fast. Her determined touch and the look in her brown sugar eyes was sweeter than all the peaches in Georgia. Now that he'd grasped what he was feeling for her, how would he ever find the strength to leave when it was time to move on with the work she admittedly understood was his passion? He placed his hand atop hers, squeezed lightly to assure her he was fine with the circumstances and then left the room.

Claire watched Daniel take charge of the meeting as if it were one of his crime scenes.

"I've already run a check on Scott Rambling and he's just a small-time crook," Daniel announced to the group. "Looks like he has a record dating back a ways, nothin' too exciting. Went straight for a while with his duplication business, when he saw his company going under he raised some money from his clients and then skipped the state. We'll track him down but he seems to operate on his own."

"So we're just supposed to assume Dawson had nothing to do with it? Look the other way and hope we're not being strung along like those churches in Sacramento?" Moe grumbled.

"Moe, part of your value to this congregation over the years is your natural tendency to play devil's advocate." Ken paid the old guy a backhanded compliment. "You've saved us from many a bad decision that way. But that's not neccssary today. Our contract is with Praise Productions, not Rambling Records. So far we have no reason to question Luke's integrity. In fact, it's just the opposite. From what I've seen everybody involved in this project is pleased as punch and can't wait for next weekend. Now let's move on to a vote so I can finish Val's chicken-fried steak in time for the first pitch of the Astros game."

When the meeting ended Claire lagged behind to be the last to personally thank Ken and Daniel for their support. She felt her face grow warm when the two men smiled their understanding and the pastor asked her to communicate their decision to Luke, rightly assuming she'd go straight and find him.

It was well past lunchtime according to her rumbling tummy. There was plenty of unfinished work at the dealership but Luke was becoming more important than all of her business details would ever be. She couldn't wait to see his face when she told him what Daniel had already uncovered. As she crossed the nearly empty parking lot the door of the Praise Productions trailer swung wide.

The dark look of worry across Luke's face zapped her spirit, flattening it like an old tire. When had her emotions become so dependent upon his? And after he was gone, how would she rekindle the comfort she'd once found in being alone with just her pets for company? She inhaled a deep breath and smiled brightly for the man who was capturing her heart.

"What would you like me to bring for supper to-night?" she called, still twenty feet from his rig.

"Tonight?"

"Sure. I have work to do this afternoon, but I'll be back at the usual time." She closed the space between them and climbed the steps to stand face-to-face.

"Are you sayin'…" He waited.

"Yep. I'm sayin'." She gently placed her left hand on the side of his neck, intentionally touching that place she knew was as much a scar on his soul as it was on his body.

"The council voted to allow you to continue the project." With her right hand she reached up to cup the back of his neck and drew his lips down to meet hers.

The intimate moment was a silent celebration of personal triumph. She released him and stepped around him entering the studio, his private sanctuary. She ran her hand along the smooth edge of the custom-built cabinet that supported a wall of high-tech sound and recording equipment. She inhaled the mellow scents of pine and lemon oil mingled with a hint of glass cleaner.

A rough-hewn limestone cross hung above the door that was set in a wall covered with framed photos of young people who posed with their instruments. It was a gallery of Luke's pupils.

One large, high-backed leather chair had rolled

away from the work console where a disposable coffee cup waited for his return. Everything was well organized, neat as a pin. The man took care of his stuff just like he took care of the kids in his life.

"What do you think?" he asked.

It wasn't the moment she'd imagined. But the answer flowed from her freely, emotions warm and expanding that had to exceed the boundaries of her heart or burst with the pressure. She crossed the carpeted floor between them and slid her hands around his waist as she pressed her cheek against his solid chest.

"I think you are the most special man I have ever known," she whispered.

He was silent. Only the quick intake of his breath told her he'd heard her soft words. His long arms snaked around her body and folded her tightly to him. They stood in the still embrace for long seconds with only the humming of the bulbs overhead to invade the quiet. She felt a shiver run through his body and heard him pull in a deep, steadying breath. She lifted her head, wanting to see his handsome face. His eyelids were closed, pressed against the light. His lips were clamped. His chin quivered.

She brushed the back of her hand along the ridge of his jaw and then pressed her palm softly to his cheek. He opened his eyes. The green of his irises had darkened to that of a shady forest.

"Oh, sugar, I don't know why," was his hushed reply.

"What a silly thing to say." She smiled to brighten the moment that, to her surprise, seemed painful for him. "Probably for lots of the same reasons that other people feel that way about you, but for a few private ones, too. And I'm standing by you no matter what some others might say."

He pulled her close, kissed the top of her head, and clutched her to his heart as if memorizing the moment for another time. She waited, hoping he would speak, knowing he was never shy about saying what was on his mind, disappointed when he didn't do so at that moment. But she interpreted his surge of emotion as a positive sign.

She had to.

He broke the embrace and set her away, turning quickly to stroke the back of his hands across his eyes. When he faced her again the lazy smile was weak but back in place. He clapped his hands once, rubbed them together and quipped, "So, what was that question you asked before? Something about my favorite subject. Supper."

Luke's concentration was shot. He'd hardly heard a note the Sons played all afternoon. Claire's declaration of support was hands down the most endearing moment of his life. And he had to go and spoil it by getting choked up. Good grief!

To make matters worse, he hadn't seized the moment. He hadn't shared his heart, told her he loved her.

Couldn't.

The memory of Lisa Evans might be covered by mental cobwebs but it was not forgotten. She'd made a similar claim, to be there for him professionally, no matter what. And when his world caved in she'd moved on in search of bigger fish. It was just a minor legality that she took most of his material worth with her.

He shrugged off the thought of his former agent, believing that other than being a well-educated career women she had nothing else in common with Claire.

Claire. She deserved so much more that a washed-up rocker with an ugly scar on his throat and a crazy life on the road. Since their conversation about him hanging around Houston he'd thought of little else. He'd made pages of notes about settling his business in one spot, and then immediately dismissed the plan as too dangerous to consider seriously. As long as he stayed mobile his past wouldn't catch up with him. Wouldn't contaminate the lives of the kids and the woman he wanted more than anything to protect.

No, if he settled down it was only a matter of time before history came calling. One day he'd turn around and Arthur O'Malley or somebody else of his ilk would recognize some remnant of Striker that wasn't buried deeply enough. The way he held a guitar, raised a mic to his lips, sang with his eyes closed. Things Luke had given up forever but missed with all his might, only dreamed about in moments of deepest sleep.

"How was that, Luke?" Chad waited, apparently for a reaction of some sort.

Luke's head snapped up at the question, his focus on the conversation hours earlier interrupted by the young male voice. The lack of understanding on his face must have given him away. Chad rolled his eyes and looked toward the others.

"See, I told you he wasn't listening."

"Hey, man," Zach called from behind his drums. "What's with you today? If we daydreamed through practice like that you'd be on us like a chicken on a June bug."

Luke was busted. The question was whether to admit it and take the heat or try to bluster past it. Before he could decide they took it out of his hands.

"Oh, he's all about Miss Claire these days. Doesn't have much blood left in his brain for us," Brian sniped.

"Cut it out, Brian," Eric admonished his brother.

"Why? We've only got a few days left and Luke's spaced out, about as interested in us as the old man is when he's sober."

Eric crossed the stage, closing the space between them in four strides of his long legs. He jammed his index finger in his brother's chest as he spoke. "Don't you ever compare Luke to the old man again, you hear me? Luke would never hit a woman or talk filthy to his kids. He wouldn't," Eric insisted as he shoved his brother with the heel of his hand.

"Yeah, he'd just steal money from churches."

The two began to scuffle, throwing and dodging punches. Their guitars, hung around their necks by leather straps, clanged together, the bashing of the strings like angry demons racing from the subwoofers.

Zach dropped his sticks and hopped off the drum platform as Chad raced toward the battling teens.

Luke vaulted up onto the front of the stage and pushed between the boys. "Hey, you two! Cut it out!"

"Tell him it's a lie, Luke," Eric pleaded, his voice choked with anger. "You weren't part of that scam in California, were you?"

"No, of course not. Let's sit down and talk about this."

Brian gave Eric a final shove and Eric popped his younger sibling with an open palm to the side of his head. The fight was on again with all four boys throwing punches.

"Stop it! Stop it right now!" Luke shouted. He'd never so much as raised his voice to a kid and here he was yelling at the boys he was learning to love like they were his own. "I'm sorry. We should have talked about this when you first got here but I've had some other stuff on my mind today."

"Gee, thanks for the undivided attention. So much for your promises." Zach spoke the words, but Luke could see from their faces that they shared the sentiment. And rightly so. He'd fallen short on his end of the deal and it was up to him to heal the wound he'd inflicted upon their relationship. He motioned for them to sit and they grudgingly complied.

"In a nutshell, I was recommending a duplication house that turned out to be crooked. I know the guy did some reputable work in the past because he got good reviews from people I trust. But he fell into financial trouble and took some money from churches who'd invested in his business. I'd love to get my hands on the guy myself, but that wouldn't help matters. So I'm going to pay back the losses instead."

"So you're admitting it was your fault?"

It was more accusation than question. The deep crease between Eric's eyes where he pulled his brows together broadcast the pain of spotting a possible flaw in his new hero. Luke's gut churned with the worry the boy's feelings heaped on a plate already full of concerns.

"No, son, I'm admitting I gave a poor recommendation that cost my clients some financial hardship. So I'm doing the right thing and making up the losses."

"Isn't that the same as when big stars and famous athletes settle with people who accuse them of stuff so they can keep their names out of the papers?"

Luke struggled against his body's desire to shudder at Eric's directness. But the kid was right. There was not much difference at all.

"Basically, yes. I don't want Praise Productions damaged by bad publicity, but more importantly those clients are my friends, just like the folks at Abundant Harvest are my friends. If I found out something bad happened to you as a result of your association with me, I'd wanna make things right. Remember, there's a youth praise band at each one of those churches and they recorded with me just like you're about to do. I'll always care about those kids just like I'll always care about you guys."

"Yeah? Well, when was the last time you talked to any of them?" Eric demanded.

"The day we said goodbye," Luke admitted.

"If they're your friends and you care so much about them, how could you leave like that?" Chad insisted.

"Oh, come on, guys. Don't lay a guilt trip on me. This is my job. Traveling is how I make my living. You can't hold that against me."

Angry faces fell and words were no longer necessary. Luke could see for himself what this was all about. He was leaving in a week. They all knew it. Claire had been right. There would be nobody to fill the gap when he was gone.

Nobody for the Harvest Sons.

Nobody for Claire.

Nobody for Luke Dawson.

"Guys, we have a recording session on Saturday. You've done a super job until now. Don't let this get you down or it will all have been for nothing."

"I don't know, Luke. My heart's just not in it right now."

"What can I do to change that, Zach?"

The normally cocky kid was pensive, head down, thinking it over. A smile played at the edges of his mouth as he looked up. "We could do a live show like we did for our audition instead of a recording in a studio. That's something I could get pumped for."

"Yeah! Stellar idea, Zach," they chorused.

"I don't know," Luke squinted as he seriously considered the change. "The logistics of a live recording are much more difficult and you can never be sure of the sound quality. Besides, I'd have to cancel the studio and hire a stage crew and we'd have to get an audience lined up."

"That's okay. We'll help with the details and work extra hard to pull it off," Eric insisted.

"There's so much that can go wrong guys, and this may be your only shot at a recording. Are you sure you want to go with such a risky setup?"

Luke looked to each band member for a vote. All gave thumbs-up to the plan.

"Okay," he agreed. "A live concert it is, then."

Chapter Twelve

The phone rang, releasing a chill that seemed to spring from Claire's core and radiate to the tips of her fingers and toes. She was alone in her office, going over the figures she'd been keying into custom spreadsheets all afternoon. The building was locked up tighter than a new hatband and the security system was armed, but being the only person inside the dealership was always a little unnerving.

"Claire Savage," she spoke into the phone.

"Hey, good lookin'."

Warmth flooded her cheeks at the sound of Luke's voice. How could such a simple compliment cause a woman who'd jumped head first into a male-dominated business to blush like an awkward fifteen-year-old at her first high school social? Heat corkscrewed through her body, chasing away the memory of the chill.

"Back atcha." She made an effort to sound cool. "Long day, huh?"

She thumped the eraser end of her pencil against the papers on her desk. "I kinda lost track of time."

"We've missed you the last couple of evenings."

"I still plan to come by. I just have to close up here and then I'll head that way. Unless you're finished for the night."

He laughed into the receiver. "Oh, no. We'll be here a good long while, but we're taking a break for about an hour. The guys have been at it all afternoon and they needed a breather."

"That sounds like something I could use since I'm the one turning out the lights tonight."

"You're not there all by yourself, are you?"

"Yes, but I do this all the time." She glanced up at the security monitor on her wall. The screen was divided into four quadrants, each flashing camera angles from various points on the property. The showroom, design shop and repair dock were dark and empty. Lights blazed in the parking lot where her beloved old Wagoneer was angled close to the front entrance.

"Want some company?"

The figures before her blurred together like a love letter left out in the rain. She breathed through the surge of thumping inside her rib cage. Ten hours ago she'd told Luke how special he was to her. Would he pretend it hadn't happened? Could she bear the brush off if he did? Either way, she'd have the rest of her life to deal with the rejection if it came to that. Heaven knew her father had given her enough practice.

Tonight Luke wanted to keep her company, without a busload of kids, a roomful of young musicians or a menagerie of pets to distract them. She wouldn't follow in her mother's footsteps and pray for God's intervention while the man she wanted walked away. Claire intended to have her say, to do everything possible to keep Luke from leaving.

"Absolutely," she answered.

Bright headlights arched across the asphalt as Luke's truck swung into the parking lot ten minutes later. Claire turned from the security monitor to survey her image in the full-length mirror behind her door. She kept an ensemble in her coat closet for emergencies. Now, her quick change into the lightweight wool slacks and matching cotton blouse transitioned her nicely from end-of-the-day-worn-out to refreshed and, she hoped, appealing.

The wad of building keys jangled in her hand and her heels clicked in time with her heartbeat as she hurried toward the front showroom. She slowed as she emerged from the darkened hallway and stopped to watch Luke approach the wide glass doors. She'd admired the male physique from a distance all of her life, never wanting to do more than observe. But this man had so captured her spirit that she finally wanted to know more, to hold and be held, to experience the physical comfort of even the most chaste contact with this man she respected.

Just as she'd changed into fresh clothing for him, he'd discarded his Praise Productions shirt in favor of a long-sleeved green pullover the same intense color as his eyes. He sported dark denim jeans and in place of his scruffy sneakers there were well-worn leather boots. If her pulse was racing at the thought of Luke before, it was taking a NASCAR turn around the track now.

She took a small step forward, the sophisticated security system detected her movement, and the showroom lit up like Times Square on New Year's Eve. Luke's charming smile crept across his face as he spotted her in the distance. He held up a white fast-food sack, rubbed his abdomen with his other hand and then pointed her way.

"We have got to stop meeting like this," she shouted as she punched the security code on the keypad by the entrance, inserted the key to release the series of deadbolt locks and pulled the door open.

He crossed the threshold, stopping to stare down into her eyes.

She took a step back and ducked her face from the intensity of his gaze. "I'm going to be fat as a possum if I don't break the habit of eating this late."

His knuckle brushed the soft skin beneath her chin as he gently guided her head upward, her eyes once again seeking his. "You have nothing to worry about. You're a whisper of a woman who can certainly afford a couple of tacos."

"Tacos?" Her eyes widened, still suspicious, expecting payback for her crime the first night they'd met.

He tipped his head back and laughed, the motion exposing his throat and the tender places she'd like to touch.

"Yeah, you'd best be concerned," he teased. "Sooner or later all chickens come home to roost, but the payback won't be anything this obvious." He shook the sack in her face.

Luke crossed to the front cashier station and deposited the sack atop the glass counter. "No, tonight my intentions are pure. I didn't want to show up empty-handed and I figured if a girl was hungry, tacos would be more welcome than yellow roses."

"Okay, if you insist." She scooped up the sack and motioned for him to follow her. "I have a fridge with drinks in my office." She flipped on lights to illuminate their path through the building and into the cozy space she had created for herself. Where the office had once been masculine in its dark woods and earth tones, now it was flooded with light. The walls and intricate crown molding were the color of heavy cream. The room was decorated with jewel-toned textured paintings, a deep comfy sofa and chairs. The cherry partner's desk was topped by a thick sheet of glass with a few cherished family photos displayed beneath its smooth surface. Only the tree-of-life Persian carpet remained as a vivid reminder of the former owner and Claire's mentor in the business.

She placed bottles of chilled mineral water on the table in the sitting area and offered Luke a chair before dropping onto the sofa and digging into the sack.

"I have to give you credit. As usual your instincts and timing are perfect. I've hardly eaten today and really did need something in my stomach." She bit into the shell, her eyes sliding closed as she chewed, enjoying the bursts of spicy flavor.

The sofa shifted as his weight dropped onto the cushion beside her. She peeked through her lashes to find him solemn-faced, elbows resting on his knees, his hands folded.

"Did something else happen, Luke?" She pushed the food aside, her hunger ignored, her blood flow slowing.

"Yes," he said softly. "*You* happened, and I had to let you know how much it meant to me. It's been a long time since anybody stuck up for me like you and Pastor Ken did today and I won't ever forget it. I really care about the people I work with and having you two believe in me means a lot."

So, in the same breath he was saying he cared about her *and* Ken Allen. How was she supposed to interpret that?

He reached across the sofa cushion and offered his hand, palm up. Claire noted, not for the first time, that this man was a gentleman to the core, always extending himself, never assuming or demanding anything from her, even in his most gruff moments. Without hesitation, she placed her hand in his, their fingers entwined.

"God really blessed me with you, Claire."

"I feel the same," she whispered.

"And I need to tell you not to worry about me." He held up his other hand when she started to protest. "Don't even try to deny it. You're the worrying kind. You worry about your parents and your business and all your employees. You worry about everybody at the church and every stray animal that crosses your path. You worry about finances and security and you worry way too much about how you look, which is just your way of hiding all your other worry."

A jolt from the truth of what he said zapped her system in the same way she'd been shocked as a child by sticking a hairpin in a wall socket. Every cell of her body surged with the reality of it, but it was not something she wanted to worry about now. And there she went, worrying about what she had to worry about later.

As if he'd read her mind, he smiled. "Right on target, huh?"

She nodded and glanced down at their hands, feeling rather foolish for being so transparent. She'd prided herself on masking her feelings for so many years that now it was embarrassing to have a man see through her this easily. Especially a man who invoked feelings so new and so raw that it was difficult to examine, even in private.

"I couldn't help being concerned when I saw how upset you were this morning," she said.

"But that was this morning. Since then I've talked with all three of the pastors who fell for Rambling's scam and offered to donate the same amount they lost."

"Have you considered that some people might see that as an admission of guilt? That might be harder on your reputation than fighting the charges."

"That's what the boys said tonight, and the bottom line is my reputation has seen worse days and by the grace of God I survived. I've made up my mind, Claire. I'm paying back the losses."

"I had a feeling you'd insist on doing that." She stood and crossed to her desk. She picked up a spreadsheet and eyed the friendly numbers, familiar symbols that never let her down.

"Luke, my investment broker faxed some information to me today. I've checked and double-checked and I can do this, so please listen to me."

She knew what his answer was likely to be. She'd prayed for the right way to extend the offer. Prayed that he could receive it without insult, see that there were no strings attached.

Luke shifted on the sofa cushion, uncertain of what was coming next. He was accustomed to moving fast in business, keeping a hectic pace to meet deadlines and travel dates. But these new matters, matters of the heart, were moving toward him at warp speed, drops of rain in a hurricane-force wind. Pelting him hard, leaving him cold, wet and shivering. He was locked out of the comfort zone that would never again be his refuge.

Instead of returning to her place on the sofa, she knelt before him, laid the legal-size paper facedown on the floor and took both of his hands in hers. She closed her eyes, paused for several long seconds and he knew she was praying. What could she possibly have to tell him that needed God's intervention?

"I want to loan you the money to repay those losses."

His head snapped back like Brian's had when Eric popped his brother on the chin. "Are you crazy?"

At the speed of sound he regretted his choice of words. Just the same, she laughed.

"Kinda."

Thank You, Lord, that she has a sense of humor.

"I'm crazy about you, but that has nothing to

do with the money. Luke, I can afford this. Let me do it."

"No!" He shook his head. "No way. Claire, I'm humbled that you would want to help me like this, but I can manage by myself."

"How? How will you come up with that kind of money? Sell your equipment to protect your name? Don't let your pride put you out of business, Luke."

"Look, you just told me a few nights ago how tight everything is for you this year and that your future depends on what happens in Sturgis. Where are you gonna get that kind of cash?"

She hesitated for a moment, maybe while she decided how much of her business she wanted to expose, then glanced up at him through spiky platinum bangs.

"It's from my investment account, money I earned from those dairy endorsements. I wouldn't put my employees' security in jeopardy, and Mama's house is paid for. This is my money under the mattress, so to speak. My seed money for a new product line if the Southern Savage isn't successful."

"Which is exactly why you're gonna leave it right where it is. That's your recovery money in case this place goes south, and you're a smart businesswoman to have it put away. I won't accept it, Claire, and that's final. I can work this out alone."

She let go of his hands, her shoulders sagged and

she dropped from her knees to sit on the floor, head and eyes downcast. Her body language was pure defeat. It was a posture he'd thought her incapable of until this moment. The same look on another female might be a ploy to get her way, but he knew better in this case.

This was Claire Savage. A woman who didn't back down.

He eased off the couch and sat on the floor beside her. She still didn't look up at him. He draped an arm around her, pulled her close and leaned his cheek against the top of her head.

"Thank you."

"For what?"

"For coming to my rescue twice in one day. Nobody's ever done that for me, Claire." He released her and leaned away so he could read her face, see into her eyes. "Do you understand? Nobody."

"But you don't want my help."

"That's not what I said. Not wanting your money and not wanting your help are two very different things. I've managed quite nicely by myself on the road for years. But this week I don't know what I'd have done without you.

"You know that state campaign that says Texas is like a whole 'nother country?" He waited while she nodded. "Well, Abundant Harvest is like a whole 'nother experience. The openness of the people, the hard work of the kids, the acceptance, welcome and support are all a shade above what I'm used to. And you've been behind so much of that. To be honest, I'm starting to wonder how I'll manage the next job without you."

Fat, shiny tears welled in her eyes. Oh, now he'd gone and made her cry. Why was it that whenever a guy tried to say something sensitive to a lady he got tears for his trouble? But this reaction from Claire was far from standard. She was poised, calm, practiced at dealing with any situation with aplomb. He knew instinctively, as with the first time she'd taken his hand, she was showing him a part of her that was best kept deeply buried. In this respect they were so much alike.

"So, you're still planning to leave?" There was a slight waver in her voice as she tilted her head toward the ceiling and blinked several times to quell the unwanted emotions.

"I have to." And he did.

She exhaled, blowing the breath of resignation upward, then looked him directly in the eye. With her emotions once again in check, she rested her palm along his jaw. "I want you to know my feelings for you will never change."

A spurt of disbelief in the form of laughter bust from his chest. He had no doubt she meant what she said, but her ignorance was bliss. She'd given him absolution for his sins without knowing the extent of them. But then others long before her had conveniently forgotten similar pledges once the chips were down. He didn't want to be around the day Claire's loyalty was tested.

"Pretty funny, huh?" She smiled and shook her head at what was certainly an odd reaction to a woman's promise of support.

"Pretty amazing." He lowered his face and covered her mouth with his own. The words from her lips were bittersweet on his tongue. Her sigh of contentment as she molded her body to his was a warm invitation to tell her how he felt. As much as he wanted to it would be wrong.

The phone on her desk jangled. He felt a pang of loss as she pulled away.

"That's probably the guys letting me know they're ready to get started again."

"You told them you were coming here?" She passed a hand through her hair, smoothed the front of her blouse and took her seat on the couch as if nothing had happened. She seemed fully recovered from the intensity of the moment, once again a cool competitor. It was no wonder she'd been at home on the Miss America stage.

"Oh, sure," he admitted casually. "They've figured out how I feel about you." He stood as she signaled for him to answer the ringing line.

Claire watched with fascination as his shield slipped back into place during the brief phone conversation. By the time he'd barked a list of orders at

Zach and Eric, he was safely behind the brusque exterior.

So, the boys knew how he felt, huh? When would he tell her how he felt? When he said goodbye?

"There's been a little change in plans," he said after dropping the handset into its cradle.

"Oh, yeah?" She bit into the cold taco, now as appealing as a mouth full of wet cardboard.

"The Sons want to record live instead of in the studio."

Stunned by this "little change," she tossed the food back into the sack. "Is there enough time to regroup for something like that? Won't that require a professional crew?"

"Sure, but I have some local contacts I can call who will take care of everything. My big concern is for the sound quality. The acoustics at Abundant Harvest are pretty good, but open air would be better." He shook his head. "There's just no time to consider anyplace else. We'll do the performance at the church with the school kids for an audience. The guys want to play before a live crowd, so that's what I'm going to give them. This may be their only recording session, so I'm gonna do everything I can to make sure they enjoy every minute."

"You're pretty amazing yourself, you know that?" She winked and lifted her bottle of mineral water in salute.

* * *

"Claire, I'm sorry to bother you at home this morning, but you've had three calls already from that Arthur O'Malley fella." Justin apologized for intruding on her personal time after such a late night.

Sunshine slanted through the wooden blinds over the bay window in her breakfast room. The shafts of light formed bright stripes on the cool tile and all three animals were stretched out, side by side, basking in the warmth.

"Did he leave a number?" She scribbled it on the edge of the business section of her newspaper and assured Justin he'd been right to call her at home.

It must be important or Art wouldn't be trying so hard to reach her. With all the calls she'd fielded recently from reporters and radio stations, it was no surprise she was hearing from the magazine again. She hoped *Today's Times* would be interested in more details on the Southern Savage. She refilled her coffee cup, stirred in sugar substitute and squirted in her one guilty pleasure, whipped cream. As she settled back into her breakfast nook, R.C. jumped up on her lap and curled himself into an orange tabby ball.

Art picked up on the first ring.

"Wow, I didn't expect you to answer the phone yourself."

"Oh, I'm not quite that much of a big shot around here. I still carry a sack lunch and sharpen my own pencils." He chuckled. "How are you, Claire?"

"Busy," she admitted, as Tripod rested his big nose on her knee and nudged her for some attention. "The phone hasn't stopped ringing. Thank you, by the way for the wonderful article. It had just the right balance of past and present that I was hoping you'd achieve."

"Well, evidently it was not heavy enough on the past to satisfy our readers. What with all the fuss in the last few years over kids in beauty pageants, we've had a torrent of e-mail asking for a follow-up. So, my editor is saving page space in an issue next month. He wants me to dig deeper, you know, really detail your days as a young girl on the competitive circuit in Texas. What do you think?"

She shoved her cup away, sloshing coffee across the glass tabletop and the unread sections of the paper.

"I'd rather not, Art."

He paused, seemingly surprised by her response. "Do you mind telling me why?"

Actually she did, but that would only pique his interest more. He made his living as an investigative reporter and he hadn't climbed the food chain in his business by backing down or killing a story just because some woman would rather not cooperate. She lifted her eyes to the ceiling and pleaded silently for the right words.

"I've already told you everything of interest. The rest is pretty boring stuff."

"How about letting me be the judge of that?" There was amusement in his voice, a tactic she felt was meant to put her at ease.

"No, you're going to have to trust me on this. The article was perfect and anything more would be overkill."

"Claire, let me put this another way." His voice changed. He was all business. "You've caught my editor's attention. He wants a detailed accounting on the perils of being a child in the spotlight. Your experience on the beauty queen treadmill is something different from the usual sitcom-kids-run-amuck scenario, and he's decided on you for the centerpiece of the story. If you don't want to cooperate, that's your call. But the piece is scheduled and we'll get what we want with or without your involvement."

She tensed in the kitchen chair, balled her free hand into a fist and dug her nails into her palm. The hand that held the portable receiver shook, bumping the cool plastic against her ear. Sensing her agitation, R.C. jumped to the floor and scurried out of the kitchen.

"Is that a threat, Mr. O'Malley?"

"No, it's simply the truth."

"And if I refuse to cooperate?"

"Look, Claire, it's not that hard to find somebody who will tell everything they know about you just to see their name in print. I've already got what I need, so why don't you save both of us some time by confirming the rumors I've heard about a former voice coach."

Her skin crawled at the thought of Arthur O'Malley knowing her shameful secret. Even worse, he assumed saving a little time was more important to her than guarding her privacy.

"I expected to be treated as a professional when I agreed to the first interview." She bristled at his threat.

"Oh, spare me the righteous indignation," he chuckled softly, obviously amused by her reaction. "You knew the reputation of the 'Out of the Spotlight' feature all along. You admitted you did it for the money, and it's time to pay the piper."

She closed her eyes and imagined the lead in on the local evening news.

"In an embarrassing feature story released by Today's Times *magazine, former Miss Texas and local entrepreneur Claire Savage was exposed by a receptionist in the office of the therapist who's treated Savage for years for the sexual abuse she suffered at the beginning of her competitive career."*

The young, up-and-coming newscaster would flash an artificially white grin for the camera, smug in the warm cocoon of her own protected, self-confident existence.

Claire had never known that world herself, and now the one she'd crafted so carefully threatened to dissolve as quickly as the packet of sweetener had melted in her steaming cup of morning coffee.

Chapter Thirteen

Luke plucked four ones from his wallet and waited patiently for his turn before the cashier.

"Good morning, Luke." The barista behind the counter waved a cheery greeting. "The usual?"

"Yes, thanks, Britti."

"You got it." The friendly young woman turned back to her work. "You're running pretty late today. I'd just about given up on you."

He glanced at the big wall clock and noted the time. Nearly ten. Hours later than his usual coffee run. But he'd needed solitude to think over Claire's incredible offer of help the night before. The urge to tell her how he felt was almost overpowering. But he'd limited his feelings to those of gratitude with no mention of the love he so wanted to share with her.

Luke paid the cashier and dropped the remaining bill and change into the tip jar.

"See you tomorrow?" Britti called.

"You betcha."

He settled sunglasses on his nose, adjusted his baseball cap and lifted the steaming cup to his lips. He sipped cautiously and turned toward the spot where his truck was parked. As the tasty latte slid down his throat he spotted the pink Mustang and sucked in a breath of recognition, sputtering in surprise.

"I'm sorry," Claire apologized as she climbed from her pony coupe. "When you weren't at your apartment, I tried the church and Ken said you might be here. He told me to remind you about his scone, by the way."

Luke snapped his fingers as he remembered his offer to pick up a pastry for the pastor, then smiled a greeting to the blonde before him, who was sweeter than any confection in the bakery. But she remained straight-faced. No hint of humor touched her eyes. As she neared his side she reached for him as a child reaches for a comforting hug. He opened his arms and she stepped inside his embrace. He felt her shudder as she sighed and relaxed against him, the stress from her worries passing out of her slender body while she drew strength from the contact.

"What is it, sugar?"

"I feel like such a fool," she muttered, her face pressed against his chest. "I thought I could strike a deal, do my part and believe God would control everybody else."

He patted her back with his free hand and took care not to slosh his drink. "I don't know what kind of deal you're talking about, but sometimes we're better off avoiding tight spots altogether instead of hoping for divine intervention to save the day."

"Yeah, but it's a little too late to apply that wisdom now."

"You wanna tell me what this is all about?"

She lifted eyes that pleaded for understanding. "Can we go sit inside and talk?"

"Would you rather follow me to the church or your office?"

"No." She shook her head emphatically, a cascade of hair brushing her shoulders. "I don't want to infect any place special with this conversation."

His skin prickled at her choice of words. If what she had to say would taint the very atmosphere surrounding them, how would the news affect him? He shrugged off the selfish thought and prepared to help her unburden from whatever troubled her so deeply. He held the door for Claire as they made their way to a corner booth in the nearly empty shop. He slid into the opposite seat and waited. She fiddled with her car keys, studying each closely as if one of the keys would unlock the answer to her problem.

Luke put his hand over Claire's to still the agitated act and stared intensely until her eyes met his.

"Just tell me," he calmly instructed.

Her stomach was a churning mass of raw nerves. She closed her eyes against the memory she'd spent half her life trying to erase. The darkness behind her lids was never enough to dim the light that had blazed on the ceiling of her mind's eye for so many years. She'd focused on that light overhead as a distraction from the secret act that had been committed against her. She didn't require the threats from the male voice instructor. Her shame was enough.

"Th-there was a voice teacher early in my competitive career. He was the best, c-came highly recommended." She slipped into the stammer that accompanied her speech anytime she communicated the memories with her therapist.

"He c-coached me at his home for a couple of months." She forced herself to look Luke in the eye, willing him to understand so she wouldn't have to say the words. "We were always alone."

His eyes narrowed, his jaw tightened, he nodded.

She looked away, hesitated for so long that he squeezed her hands, encouraging her to continue.

"I'm so ashamed of what happened, Luke. I was too young to understand. M-my mother never expected anything like that so she h-hadn't prepared me, didn't warn me." She searched for the words, hating to speak of it with Luke.

"But you told her, right?"

She shook her head. "Not for a long time."

He closed his eyes and dropped his chin to his chest.

"Claire." There was anguish in the way he said her name. And just like before, she felt it was all her fault.

She'd endured the humiliation for weeks, silently accepting her fate, believing the teacher who told her this was her due for being a young temptress.

"When I finally told Mama I begged her not to go to the police." Claire's voice was no more than a whisper. She moved her lips to get the words out but forced little air along with the syllables, hoping to keep them from clinging to her, clinging to Luke.

"By then Daddy was long gone and we were on our own. I knew what kind of fuss there would be. I'd had a couple of important wins and Mama and I had mapped out our plans. Public embarrassment would have cost me my education."

Luke stared at the tabletop. Slowly, unbelievably he shook his head. "And your mother just let the jerk get away with that?"

"Not on your life." Claire always felt a measure of pride at the memory of how her mother had confronted the man. "She threatened him with physical alteration if he ever came near me again."

There was a small puddle of shredded napkin on the table between them, the result of her need to destroy something as she told the story, as if by tearing apart the paper she could do the same to the memories. Luke swept it aside and took both of her hands in his once again. The warmth of his skin was a balm, soothing the icy chill that had settled over her spirit.

"You're incredibly brave to tell me this when you didn't have to, but it does explain some things."

"I'm not telling you just so you'll understand me better. There's more." Now he was going to find out what a fool she really was. Seeming world-savvy, Luke would probably never put his private life at risk by doing something as stupid as what she'd done. He'd even tried to warn her against it. But the worst was out. Only the ignorance and backlash of her decision remained.

"*Today's Times* is determined to do a feature next month on the perils of being a private kid in the public spotlight. They want something apart from the sitcom tragedies of the eighties and the editor seems to think I'm the perfect subject."

Luke's jaw tensed as he ground his teeth. "This is all O'Malley's doing, isn't it?"

"Not entirely." She felt lame defending the man, but it really was her own fault. Mama always said when you pick up a snake you should expect to get bitten. "The editor had the idea for the feature, but O'Malley's on to something and he's going to get his story with or without my help."

"Oh, sugar." Luke leaned his head against the tall padded back of the booth and closed his eyes. "I knew the moment I recognized the guy that he was bringing something bad into our lives."

Our lives. He saw this as his problem, too. Her spirit lifted for the first time that day.

Thank You, Father, that Luke isn't rejecting me because I'm damaged goods, that he cares enough to feel my worries as though they were his. For just a moment her heart felt lighter. Then she realized what he'd said.

"You recognized O'Malley?"

"Uh, yeah, when you brought him into the church that night." His words rushed out. "I knew I'd heard his name somewhere before. He's pretty big in print journalism, ya know."

"And you tried to warn me." She hung her head.

"Hey." His fingers tightened on hers. "It was just a hunch and I could have been wrong."

"But you weren't, and now look what a mess I could be in."

"Maybe not." The distracted tone of Luke's voice said he was mulling over the subject.

Her gaze darted upward. "What makes you say that?"

"Let me think about this today, I may have an idea."

Her head throbbed with the problem. She disentangled her fingers from Luke's and massaged her temples with the heels of both hands. "I'm going to give this to God. There's nothing else I can do anyway."

With his pulse pounding at the base of his throat,

Luke watched Claire pressing her hands to her head, as if she were trying to squeeze the fear from her mind. The worry emanated from her like waves of heat, searing his skin and sinking into his soul.

A small, unwanted thought started low in the depths of his consciousness and spiraled upward, determined to surface no matter how he tried to ignore it. In the span of a few seconds it was a fully formed plan that was fated to change the course of his life. But could he go through with it? For the precious, unselfish woman across the table from him, yes, he would make the sacrifice.

He loved Claire. The feeling was a deep, pure emotion he'd never known before and may never experience again. No matter the future, he would carry his feelings for her for the rest of his days. So her problems were his problems, but how could he tell her that? How could he help without tipping the hand he was trying so hard to keep to himself? He couldn't change the past, but surely he could do something that would make a difference for her future. Something to help her hate him less after he was gone.

He adjusted his cap, repositioned the sunglasses over his eyes and stood with his hand out to Claire.

"You're right. As Christ said, worry won't add a single day to your life." Luke pulled her to her feet, admiring the faith of the woman who stood before him. "I have a lot to do today and if you'll give me some help I think I can keep you too busy to worry about this."

Grateful eyes sought his. "Thank you, Luke. That's all I really wanted to hear you say."

"No, I don't have an appointment, but please give Mr. O'Malley my card and tell him I'm prepared to wait as long as it takes to see him today. I only need a few minutes of his time."

Luke snapped his business card on the granite counter before the receptionist and then settled into a chair by the window. On a hot summer day, the vision of New York from the thirty-eighth floor of the office tower was incredible. It had been years since he'd visited the city that never sleeps. After a slow turn around the island while they awaited landing instructions from air traffic control, Luke had enjoyed the view as the aircraft approached LaGuardia.

Now he glanced down at his jeans and T-shirt. There had been no time to change. He'd rattled off a list of jobs for Claire to accomplish, made a half-dozen phone calls and then headed straight to Bush Intercontinental Airport. Luke had been telling the truth about his busy day, even if he hadn't mentioned his schedule now included the first available flight to New York.

"Luke Dawson?" The voice was unsure.

Luke stood and turned to face his old nemesis. Though it galled him to do it, he extended his hand.

A man on a mission couldn't afford to have pride or principles stand in his way.

O'Malley's eye widened as he accepted Luke's greeting. "So, it *is* you. This is quite a surprise given your reluctance to speak with me in Houston."

Luke withheld the expected apology. "I'm a busy man just as I'm sure you are. Could we speak privately? This won't take long."

"Evelyn, answer my line, please." O'Malley inclined his head in understanding and turned toward his corner office. "Right this way."

Luke fell into step behind O'Malley, a prisoner following the padre to the gallows. As he strode toward a front-end collision with the truth he prayed his decision to protect Claire at all cost wasn't one he'd have to pay for the rest of his life.

Claire sat in the sound booth next to Dana and listened for what seemed like the hundredth time as the Sons rehearsed their opening number. Dana rolled her unadorned eyes and puffed her cheeks out, evidence of her exasperation over the lackluster performance.

The guys were dragging from days of non-stop practice. On an energy level scale, theirs was at bedrock. Once the auditorium was packed with kids, that alone would build excitement, but they couldn't depend on the momentum of teenage vibes to get them through what would surely be the most important performance of their young lives. They needed to be pumped from the inside out. Each member of the band had a personal stake in the outcome of the recording and that buy-in had to be evident in every movement that accompanied the music. Without the unique synergy of the Harvest Sons on top of the enthusiasm of their audience, they were doomed.

Something was simply missing. Certainly it made a difference that Luke was out of pocket for the day, but there was more. The joy of the event had leaked out of the band as if a pinprick had released the lighter than air element that kept them flying high over this career opportunity. She watched the guys struggling with the number they could play in their sleep under normal circumstances.

What had Luke said to her only last night? *Abundant Harvest is like a whole 'nother experience.* And why shouldn't that impression carry into their recording? Why not take this unique experience to the next level? Kick it up a notch.

Claire fished her Blackberry out of its hiding place in the bottom of her shoulder bag and dialed directory assistance. Several phone calls later she punched the A/V console button that would feed her voice to the stage.

"Eric, you guys take fifteen."

"Thanks, Miss Claire, but we've gotta work through this problem with the chorus before Luke gets back or he'll skin us alive."

She smiled at Luke's familiar threat, knowing he'd probably never skinned more than his own knee.

"I think I have a suggestion that may help, but I need to speak with Pastor Ken first. So you guys grab a soda and relax. I promise I'll have something encouraging to share with you when I get back."

When they waved agreement she turned to Dana. "You take a break, too. It's been a long day for everybody but I think it's about to get exciting again."

Dana's eyes narrowed. "What are you up to, Miss Claire?"

"That obvious, huh?" She smiled at the girl who was looking like a Gap commercial in her khaki slacks, polo shirt and trendy pink high-top sneakers.

"Oh, yeah. You had that same look in your eye the night you talked my dad into chaperoning the seventh grade ski trip."

"And didn't we have a blast riding that bus all the way to Colorado?" she insisted, then hurried down the steps of the elevated booth and made a beeline for the pastor's office.

"Ken?" she called, as she knocked on the frame of the door that was always open.

"Hey, Claire." He looked up from the materials she knew he was organizing into his next discipleship curriculum. "What's up?"

"Luke needs our help."

Ken leaned forward, waiting for details.

"He's offered to make good on the losses of those California churches."

Ken whistled at the potential amount. "But the investigation is still under way."

"Nothing I could say would make him reconsider."

"Luke shouldn't feel responsible for that money if he's completely innocent."

The pastor's words niggled at the edge of her thoughts. She hadn't slowed down enough in the days since the accusation to objectively consider Luke's determination to repay the losses. He couldn't possibly feel guilty in some way, could he? Was he insisting on making restitution because the damage *was* somehow his fault?

"Should we check with Daniel, find out if there's any news on the investigation?" she asked.

"He said he'd call as soon as he had anything." Ken shook his head, waved away her concern. "No, I've got a good sense about Luke. From what I've seen of him, it doesn't really surprise me that he feels responsible, whether he is or not. He's a straight shooter and in his mind this may be the only way to handle a situation when people he cares for are involved." Ken angled his head and gave her a pointed look. "You couldn't do much better than a man like Luke Dawson."

"I get the hint." She grinned weakly, knowing sadness and now confusion laced the smile. "Unfortunately, that's not up to me."

"How can I help this along?"

"I don't know that there's much you can do on that subject. Luke's even more private than I am so I wouldn't presume to guess how he feels about matters of the heart.

"But I do have some insight into how important his business is to him and how much he loves his work. If he has to give up what little security he has to repay those debts, I don't know how he'll continue his music ministry."

"Would he accept a loan?"

"I already went that route. He wouldn't hear of it."

Ken leaned back in his old desk chair, scratched his jaw and puzzled over the situation. Then his eyes met Claire's. "What are you thinking, young lady?"

She felt a peace settle over her that comes only from serving others. Her idea may be half-baked, but it was inspired. With an army of help, the wonderful folks of Abundant Harvest could pull it off. She was certain of it.

She was also certain that if her plan was successful she could foolishly be helping the man she'd fallen in love with to move on with his life, pushing him on his way just as if she'd packed his bags herself.

Chapter Fourteen

At two in the morning the courtesy shuttle pulled to a stop at the tailgate of Luke's heavy-duty pickup.

"Man, tough break," the driver said as he glanced down at the conspicuous orange "boot" device that held Luke's front tire prisoner.

Through the light drizzle, Luke caught sight of the "Reserved for City Official" sign posted on the fence and slapped a palm against his forehead.

"Even in a hurry, I should have known that spot was too good to be true." Luke fished a ten from his wallet and held it toward the twentysomething driver.

"Is there any chance you could take me to the impound lot so I can pay my fine and get that thing unlocked?"

"Sorry, dude, but they're closed till eight. It's the city's way of grinding a little salt in the wound."

Luke scuffed the backs of his hands over his eyes and groaned. He'd planned to wait until later in the day to break the news to Claire, but now seemed like as good a time as any. Besides, he needed a ride.

Thirty minutes later she swung her ancient Wagoneer through the circular drive of the park-and-fly lot. Beneath the portico, she stomped the brake, rolled down the window and poked out her head.

"Hey stranger, can I give you a lift?" she teased.

He leaned his elbows against the faded red truck as he lightly placed a hand on either side of her head. Even at this hour with a hectic day behind her, she was stunning. He angled his mouth over hers and kissed her more deeply than he'd ever dared before, sharing a message of longing that he could never put into words.

It was done. The price had been high but he'd saved Claire's future. Unfortunately, he had less than twenty-four hours before word of Striker's resurfacing broke. Then he might as well have a bounty on his head. Every newshound or over-thirty rock fan would be hunting him down.

Thank God the plan had worked. O'Malley had taken the bait and swallowed the hook. In exchange for *Today's Times* losing interest in Claire Savage, Luke gave an exclusive that was far bigger and more sensational than anything the publisher had imagined. If they wanted to examine the life of a kid in the spotlight, their wildest dreams had just come true.

Luke was in the driver's seat and he had some requirements that were not open for discussion. After the deal was struck O'Malley had rushed Luke two floors down to a cable news studio. He sat in darkness, his face shielded from the camera as they taped spots that would tease the listening audience. In order to learn the full story of Striker Dark's disappearance from his high-profile life in the heavy-metal music scene over a decade ago, fans would have to purchase the upcoming issue. *Today's Times* was literally stopping the presses to include the sensational scoop.

The anonymity Luke had guarded so closely would evaporate the moment his words were typeset. The ministry he'd built would collapse under the weight of his past sins. His days as low-profile business owner Luke Dawson were numbered and he could count them on one hand. Striker Dark loomed large in the shadows and he was finally about to have his moment in the sunlight again.

"Wow," Claire breathed when Luke ended the kiss. "Welcome back from wherever you've been."

He rounded the front bumper of the old truck, jumped into the passenger's seat and dumped his backpack into the floorboard as the door closed against the damp night.

"You're a life saver. Thanks for looking after Freeway today and for coming out in this crummy weather." He buckled the seat belt and folded his hands together to control the nervous fidgeting that had plagued him during the long flight.

She smiled and shrugged off the praise. "When you live in Houston you get used to summer rain. Besides, a late night drive beat anything on cable by a long shot."

He flinched at the mention of cable television, certain the spots were already being aired.

"Glad I didn't wake you."

"Oh, I have too much on my mind to be asleep anyway."

"Good stuff?" he questioned.

The tiny creases of worry that had framed her eyes earlier in the day were gone. She seemed relaxed and energized, just the opposite of what he was feeling at the moment.

"Lots of good stuff. Practice went extremely well today. I think you'll be surprised at the progress the guys made while you were gone."

"See, they can do it without me. They won't miss a beat once they're on their own, especially as long as you're still willing to help out."

Her smile faltered.

Now, why had he brought that up? With the pieces of the puzzle fitted together, he fully understood the damage his leaving would inflict upon Claire. And there was more yet to come.

She turned her attention to merging onto the dark expressway that was busy with fast-moving vehicles even at this hour. Passing her hand over the shadows of the dashboard, she twisted a knob and the windshield wipers creaked to life. The summer rain was creating a slick sheen on the steamy pavement.

"I guess they fed you on the flight from..." She waited for him to complete the sentence.

He hesitated. Was this the time? And how much should he tell her? Just enough to ease her mind, or everything? He'd prayed for the answers to those questions as the 727 jet had cruised the skies across eight states. Fate seemed to have set up this unexpected time together. Luke wondered if he was meant to take advantage of it.

Claire squinted through the windshield that always needed washing. Fat raindrops spattered against the glass before the wipers whisked them away. As sure as the storm clouds that had gathered all day dampened the city, Luke's comment had dampened her excitement over the day's whirlwind of plans. She exhaled the sadness from her lungs and fixed her prize-winning smile back in place. The goal was to help Luke. No strings attached, and certainly no guilt heaped on him for placing the work he loved above all else. Above her.

She playfully elbowed his arm to snap him out of his silent thoughts.

"Was the weather at least nicer where you went today?"

"I didn't notice."

The quiet gaze he turned on her was impossible to read in the shadows of the truck. He seemed conflicted, reluctant to talk. The grumpy-old-Luke facade that he wore with the boys was moments from scttling back into place.

She accelerated and pulled into a left-hand lane to pass the old sedan that slowed her progress.

"I went to see O'Malley," he blurted.

"In New York?" Amazed by his admission, she let off the gas pedal, her head snapping to the right.

A horn blared from behind when the Wagoneer suddenly lost speed. Claire's hand flew to the cross at her throat as she picked up the pace again. She glared in her rearview mirror at the impatient driver.

"I hate it when people do that. It scares me to death."

"Sorry, I probably should have waited till we got to the house so you could concentrate on the road."

"I actually listen and drive at the same time quite well. For a blonde," she added, making light of the abrupt announcement so he'd continue.

As they passed beneath the hazy yellow glow from a tall streetlamp, he seemed to study her face as if trying to gauge her reaction to his admission. He was silent for long seconds as he watched her, his eyes giving away the concern he must feel. And, she admitted to herself, he had reason to worry. Anyone else who'd intruded in her business would be on the receiving end of a stern lecture right now.

Anyone but Luke.

Luke was a grouchy white knight. A fixer. He made his living helping others do things better, avoid pitfalls, put their best foot forward. She should have known that pouring her heart out to him was an invitation to help her out of a dangerous spot. And considering what she and Pastor Ken were up to, she was in no position to throw stones.

"*Today's Times* seems to have lost interest in that follow-up piece on you."

Her breathing stopped. The fluttering in her chest a telltale sign of the fear she'd been holding in check all day. She took her right hand off the wheel and pressed her fingertips to Luke's forearm. His muscles were tense and rigid. His hands were clasped together in front of him, tight fists of nervous energy.

"Tell me," she said simply.

"I happen to know a lot of kids in the business, so I offered to hook O'Malley up with a pretty sensational story."

"About whom?"

"Oh, it's a guy who played heavy metal before he made the switch to contemporary Christian. I hope you won't be offended by me saying this, but—" a mischievous smile spread across his handsome face "—it'll sell a lot more magazines than your story."

She studied her mirrors before cautiously crossing two inside lanes of traffic and pulling to the side of the road. Her wheels grabbed the pavement a few feet from a concrete barrier that would shield the ever-present daytime road crew. She checked the emergency lane behind them for oncoming traffic before shoving the gearshift into Park and turning to Luke.

"I hope you know I didn't come to you this morning expecting you to do anything but listen. I can fight my own battles, Luke, I always have."

The mood of his smile shifted from playful to thoughtful as he took her hand.

"And I'm sure you'd have managed just fine on your own. But the fact of the matter is that not all battles are worth the effort. I had a hunch that if I got in front of O'Malley I could steer his sensation-seeking radar in another direction so you wouldn't need to fight at all. I'm sorry I interfered without your permission, but I couldn't sit by and watch somebody who means so much to me get hurt."

She stared at the large hands that cupped hers and waited for him to continue, hoping for an admission that his motivation came from him heart and was not the same protectiveness he showed all his kids. The rain picked up, slapping the old SUV with curtains of water, blown sideways by gusts of southern wind.

"Forgive me?" he asked.

"Anything."

He lifted his right hand and trailed it down the side of her cheek, caressing her skin with the back of his fingers. She angled her face toward the tender gesture and kissed his knuckles. Her throat tightened with the longing to tell him what she'd discovered that morning when she'd been driven to unburden herself to Luke, to turn to one person only for guidance and comfort.

She loved him.

But he wouldn't want to hear her profess the love that overflowed from her heart, couldn't return her feelings.

"Come on, sugar, but let's get out of this weather."

He turned his attention to the panels of glass that surrounded them. Layers of white were creeping up the insides, enclosing them by an opaque curtain.

"Where's your defroster?" he asked, twisting dials on the shadowy dash.

Afraid to speak over the profound sadness that thickened her voice and filled her eyes, she brushed his hand away and groped for the knob she'd twisted a bazillion times since her mother financed the used truck that was Claire's high school transportation. As the system pumped a steady supply of warm air, she clicked on her left turn signal and grabbed the steering wheel to merge into the stream of headlights. With her vision blurred by hot tears, she glanced toward her side mirror and accelerated.

The deafening blast of a horn warned there was a huge vehicle almost on top of them. She gasped from the jarring sound and jerked the wheel hard to the right, overcorrecting.

The tires spun on the slick pavement and the Wagoneer slid sideways.

Her eyes flew to the tunnel of clear vision that was spreading across the windshield just as the front quarter panel of the SUV smacked the concrete barrier.

A shotgun report roared in Claire's ears. Her face and chest stung from an immediate and powerful slap that left her skin smarting. White powder swirled about her, turning the front seat into a snow globe of confusion.

She choked on the air filled with floating debris and the warm blood that rushed from inside her lip. Feeling the surge of a gag that would bring up her dinner, she prepared to lean toward the floor of the passenger's seat.

Luke's strong left arm shot across her upper body and pinned her securely.

"Hold on, Claire. A truck stopped behind us to help."

"Luke," she groaned.

"I'm okay. Are you hurt?"

"No, but I feel like I'm gonna barf."

"You caught that air bag right in the face. Just take a few deep breaths and let your head stop spinning."

"I want to go home," she groaned.

Her door swung wide and rain pelted her through the opening.

"Don't move, little lady." The overall-clad truck driver used his large body to shield her from the weather.

"I don't think she's injured, just shook up from the air bag blast," Luke advised the trucker. "Claire, are you sure you don't want an ambulance?"

She waved away the question.

"We just need a wrecker," Luke told the trucker.

"Got it." The door closed against the downpour.

Luke leaned across the console, draped his arm around her shoulders and pulled her close. She hugged him hard, a sob springing from her throat. He kissed the top of her head and rocked her like a child.

"It was a beat-up old SUV, but it might still be salvageable."

"It's not my truck, it's you. I could have killed you."

He tipped her head and used his fingertips to brush away the tears.

"Shhh," he murmured into her hair. "I'm the proverbial cat with nine lives and I've still got a bunch left. As a matter of fact, I need to tell you about the first one so let's get you home."

"Thanks, pastor, I'll see you in half an hour," Luke said, ending the phone call. He closed his eyes and pleaded a silent prayer for the words to break the news to Claire, fearing this might be the last time they'd be together.

"I can give you a ride."

Her insistent voice brought him back to the present, where he stood shivering in her kitchen.

With four animals in tow, she emerged from the hallway that led from her bedroom and bath. She'd made a quick change into dry clothes and brought a large towel for Luke. He could wrap it around his shoulders to absorb some of the dampness in his T-shirt but there wasn't much he could do about his soaked jeans and shoes.

He stood dripping on the rug, leaning against the edge of the counter, feeling like his back was once again up against a hard place with nowhere to turn. He glanced at the wall clock, watched the sweeping hand click away the seconds as the last few moments she might ever respect him ticked away with it.

"There's no way you're getting behind the wheel without some sleep first." He refused her offer. "Ken was already up and he's going to drop by for me on his way to the church. As a matter of fact, he's a little annoyed that we didn't call him in the first place instead of riding with the wrecker."

"That's Pastor Ken, all right."

She crossed the room, shook open the beach towel, draped it around Luke's shoulders, and ran her hands down his chest to mop up the dampness. The heat of her touch was stronger than his willpower. He pulled her against him, not caring that her dry clothes would be wet in an instant. She wound her arms around his waist, hugged him hard and nestled her cheek to his chest.

"I have something to tell you, sugar."

She made to tip her head back to look him in the face, but he pressed her closer to his heart.

"No, let me hold you a little longer in case you never want to hug me again."

"It can't be that bad."

"Oh, yeah," he corrected. "It can."

She pushed away enough to see into his eyes. "Luke, whatever it is, there's nothing we can't work through."

He dipped his head, inhaled her fresh scent and kissed her softly, making a sweet memory.

"Let's sit at your table."

The animals trotted behind them to the breakfast nook and plopped on the floor at their feet. Luke covered the chair with his towel and sat, stretching his legs in front of him, creating the distance he was certain she'd want once she heard what he had to say.

"You were right. O'Malley's on to something. He knew the truth about your abuse by that creep and was prepared to ambush you with the information to get your reaction."

She closed her eyes and ducked her head, unable to bear the tender look of sympathy she saw on Luke's face. Her soul cried out for help.

Oh, Father, why are You testing me this way?

*Why now, when I'm finally getting over those hor-
rible memories? When I've found a man I can love
without shame?*

She felt the light pressure of his hand on her knee,
warm and reassuring. She opened her eyes but
wouldn't meet his gaze. Couldn't.

"I thought I'd gotten past it, survived it," she murmured to herself.

"You have. That's what I'm telling you. O'Malley has a bigger story. You're not in danger of being
exposed."

Her eyes met Luke's. He sat up tall and pulled his
long legs close to the kitchen chair. His hands were
once again pressed together between his knees, his
body language distant like he was closing off from
the world. From her.

"I know you love music but you don't seem like
the type who'd listen to heavy metal. Do you remember the band that did 'Electric Love' and 'Ain't
No Fool' and a lot of other mega hits in the 90s?"

This had to be the most bizarre twelve hours of
her life. She still felt light-headed from taking the
impact of the airbag blast to her face. Then the ordeal of loading the SUV in the pouring rain and
hitching a ride with a wrecker. Now, out of the blue
Luke wants to talk about 90s rock?

"Luke, I'm confused but I'm not stupid. Anybody under the age of eighty would know about
Striker Dark. What's he got to do with anything?"

"That's me."

She squinted, trying to make sense of the words.

"I'm Striker."

"Yeah, right. You're that guy with the long black hair and the spiderweb tattoos who…"

"Burned his face up freebasing," he finished her sentence, then tilted his head so the scars on his neck were obvious.

She held her palms outward, fed up. "I don't know where this is headed, but that's a ridiculous story, Luke."

He closed his eyes, sucked in a deep breath and shook his head as if telling himself there was no other way.

He stood, turned his back to her, peeled the long sleeves off and lifted the damp black T-shirt over his head. Luke held his arms out to give her the full view of the infamous artwork.

She felt her jaw sag at the picture he made. His back and arms were an intricate web spun by an artist's needle. A menacing spider the size of Luke's open hand so believably detailed that as he rotated his arm it appeared to crawl across his shoulder in search of innocent prey.

Striker Dark, that notorious bad boy of the 90s, standing there in her kitchen.

"Oh, my," she breathed the quiet exclamation. No wonder he didn't want Daniel Stabler digging into his past.

He dragged the shirt back on before turning to face her. "Sorry, but that was the simplest way to make you understand.

"I'm the kid who grew up in the spotlight. The person *Today's Times* is going to feature. I gave O'Malley the answers to everybody's questions about what happened to me after the fire. He's running it in this week's issue and we taped some teasers for their cable news station." He nodded toward her television. "I'm sure they're already being aired."

Her head throbbed. Her heart pounded. She dared not make any assumptions but hope overflowed her spirit.

"After all these years, why did you expose yourself like that, Luke? Why didn't you protect your reputation, your privacy?"

He moved to stand before her and knelt to one knee so they were eye to eye. He held his hands outward, palms up, an invitation. She placed her hands in his. He smiled and squeezed them lightly.

"Because I finally found someone more important to protect than myself. The woman I love." His voice was low, quiet, but there was no mistaking the words he spoke.

Blood surged through her heart, increasing the pounding in her head. Knowing it was a moment she would treasure for the rest of her days, she struggled to note the details. The damp smell of him, the appealing stubble of his day-old whiskers, the deep emerald-green of his eyes, their corners pinched with something that looked suspiciously like sadness. Why would he say the words she'd been waiting all her life to her with regret on his face?

"And that's why I have to get out of here."

She snapped out of her memory making and back to the present. What had he just said? "Get out of here? What are you talking about?"

"I need to get packed up and on the road before people see that spot and recognize my voice. Abundant Harvest will be crawling with the press if they think I'm there. I won't put Ken and the Harvest Sons through that mess."

"Oh, come on. It's been what, twelve, maybe fourteen years since all that happened? You can't really believe it's going to be that big of a deal?"

The doorbell rang. He gave her hands a final squeeze before he stood. "That'll be the pastor." Luke moved to the built-in desk and depressed the start button on her computer.

"I suggest you spend an hour surfing the net for Striker Dark. Then I think you'll have the picture of just how big a deal this is gonna be."

Chapter Fifteen

"Lord, I know You didn't bring me to this point to let my life unravel now. Show me Your will for my future, and give me the strength to accept it."

Luke ended his time of prayer and opened his eyes to the empty carton that needed to be filled with his kitchen items. The last thing he wanted to do today was pack and run but it wasn't his choice to make. Every hour that he stalled put the hounds closer to his heels.

His father had been right. Trouble seemed to find Luke wherever he went. He'd spent so many years running from it, trying to put a safe distance between him and his excessive past, always afraid one day it would catch him unaware.

The television anchor gave the afternoon weather report. Luke knew he had to get moving. He could be loaded and on the road in less than three hours if he worked fast.

Knuckles rapped softly on his front door and Freeway woofed at the intrusion.

"Luke, can I come in?" Claire called. The question caused him to suck in a quick breath of surprise as he heard uncertainty in her always-confident tone. He felt a smile of relief crease his face as the pup wagged his tail at the familiar voice.

"It's open," Luke shouted.

She peeked around the door facing, her eyes wide and filled with hesitation. Freeway loped across the room to greet their unexpected visitor. Luke held out his hand and prayed she'd still take it. She moved into his kitchen, set a bunch of yellow rosebuds in a crystal vase on the counter and slipped her fingers into his. When she gave his hand a small comforting squeeze it was like she'd squeezed his heart instead.

"I read on the Internet this morning where you once hated being confined to small spaces." She gestured to the tiny apartment.

"Been doing a little research, have you?"

She nodded. "Is all that stuff true?"

He closed his eyes, ashamed of what she might have read. Might have seen. He felt her hand press his for an answer.

"Most of it." He looked into eyes sweeter than molasses. "Striker was a character I was only supposed to play on stage. Some of his antics made Lucifer seem like a choir boy. I'd like to blame everything on Striker but all the foolish decisions and sinful behavior were mine alone."

"You look so different from the person in those pictures. It's hard to believe that was you beneath the beard and long hair."

"Most of my face looked like this after the fire." He touched the scar on the side of his neck. "I told the surgeons who did the reconstruction to change everything they could. By then I'd given my heart to Christ and I didn't want any part of that old life. I needed to start over, use my talents for His service, and I knew I'd never be taken seriously if people recognized me."

Her curious gaze roamed across his face, possibly searching for the irreverent kid he'd been all those years ago. She was too polite to ask the question on her mind so he made it easy for her.

"I was smoking cocaine, my favorite recreation back then. My shirt caught fire and all that hair was like dry tinder. By the time my buddies got me rolling on the floor to put out the flames, my skin was more like melted putty than flesh."

She winced at the blunt description that was nothing compared to the reality. The combination of rehab for drug addiction and burn recovery without pain meds was a living hell. But a hell he'd brought upon himself. Only God's grace had seen Luke through it and in gratitude he'd turned his craft into a mission field.

"Pretty stupid, huh? Not exactly the type of guy you'd want working with your kids today."

"But you've changed, Luke. Everyone will be so proud of you when they realize what you've done with your life since then."

The forgiving smile she gave him said she simply didn't get it. He snickered, a sound that was part humor at her hopeful expression and part despair at the loss yet to come. He hated what he was about to do, but there was no choice. She had to walk away, leave him behind. Put space and time between them before she was sucked under with him.

"Claire, you're living in a dream world. I'll be lucky if I don't get run out of town before I can get packed on my own and leave tonight."

Leave tonight. Leave tonight. Leave tonight His words echoed in time with the throbbing headache that still plagued her.

Claire felt light-headed, the oxygen sucked from her lungs. He had no reason to keep running. His secret was out. He said she was the woman he loved. But, just like her father, *his feelings* were all that mattered. He would go anyway.

"What about the Harvest Sons?"

"People like Moe Sanders won't let me within a hundred yards of the Sons now. No." He shook his head and then continued. "I'm not going to put everybody through that."

"You're just going to cancel their concert?"

"Of course not. I've already made some calls, and arranged for the same company who recorded the Battle of the Bands to take over. They'll make all the arrangements so the show can go on as planned."

"The church can't afford that," she protested.

"They'll charge the same rate Ken agreed to in my contract."

"You thought of everything, didn't you." She was defeated. Nothing left to lose.

"I'm trying to make everybody whole."

"Well, try harder because I'm never going to be whole again. I need you, Luke. I love you." She heard the pleading in her voice. It was sickening. It hadn't worked with her father and it wouldn't work now, either.

"I love you, too, Claire," he whispered.

The green of his eyes glittered with tears of conflict. She bit the tender inside of her lip to quell the sob that wanted to surface at his admission.

He'd said it again. He loved her.

"But nothin' good can come of it, sugar," he continued, determined to spoil any chance they had to be together. "Our lives are on completely different courses. Yours is very public. You need exposure, feed on attention. If you don't have that your business won't be successful and you won't be happy. I've gone so far underground that I'm not sure I even know how to be a public person again. Everything I touch from today on will be tainted by who I was and I can't do that to you. I won't."

"Luke, please." She tried again, her emotions raw, close to losing control. She grasped his hand with both of hers, physically trying to hold him back. He gripped her fast.

"Baby, let me say it differently." He glanced away. "I'm such a big fake that my own parents disowned me. I'm so ashamed of the person I was back then. I don't want to live in the spotlight, constantly being asked about those times, never being allowed to forget. It would be a prison for me." His gaze met hers again. "Don't you see? It's the nightmare of my past that made me see the same thing in you. I was so alone and miserable as a kid that I could easily recognize your pain. I understand your shame. I can't step back into that world again, can't be trusted with the temptations that still taunt me, will find me now."

"But you're a new creature." She tried for a Biblical approach.

"That's where you're wrong," he insisted, making the snap decision to force her at all cost to let him go, even if he had to be cruel to do it. Even if he had to lie. "When this fraud investigation is complete my name will be worthless and I'll have even more reason to go underground. I've got to put as many miles between us as I can before the truth comes out. Then I can go on hiding, and you can too. Like you've done for years."

"What's that supposed to mean?" She leaned away.

The narrowing of his eyes made her want to flinch from his gaze.

"Oh, come on, Claire. You can drop the Pollyanna act with me. We're no different in that respect. I may have been hiding behind my anonymity, but you've been hiding behind that perfect persona, that prima donna you've created for yourself, afraid one slip will justify what that jerk did to you. Confirm what you believe, that it's really all your fault."

His tactless words stung, a vicious slap to her senses.

"How can you speak to me that way?" She bristled.

"Because it's true." He mocked her. "We're the same on the inside, you and me. Afraid, hiding our sins, dirty, not even trusting God's forgiveness."

The heat of his hands was as unbearable as the hurtful words he flung at her. She jerked hers free and pushed away.

What he insinuated was a lie! Wasn't it? He couldn't possibly have stolen from people who believed in him.

And what about his accusations regarding her? Were the guilt and unworthiness she still felt a part of not really trusting God? Never truly accepting His forgiveness? How could she have been so wrong about so many things?

If what he said was true, she was as much a fake as Luke.

Self-confident business woman. Public figure. Outspoken Christian role model. Was she only an image with no substance? And had she finally placed her trust in a man—*fallen in love with a man*—who was a fraud in every sense of the word?

"You know deep down that it's all true whether you'll admit it to me or not," he spewed bitter words at her.

"Okay!" She held her hands up, demanding that he cease the verbal assault. "You've made your point. I get the message, loud and clear. And I'll pass it on to the Sons. You don't want to be in the spotlight. You're outta here because you can't chance a new life here with us. Don't have anything to offer because you're a big fake, even embezzling funds from the churches you worked with. Did I get all that right, Luke? Or Striker, or whoever you *really* are?"

She snatched the bouquet of flowers from the vase and dumped them in the metal waste basket, innocent petals and drops of water scattering on the floor as they fell.

At the door she turned and extended a challenge, now positive he'd resist it.

"The concert's been moved, by the way. It'll be at the West Houston Amphitheater. Saturday night at seven. If you're brave enough to stick around, drop by and check it out. You might be surprised by what the community you're so certain will turn its back on you is doing to help somebody out of a tough spot."

She yanked the door hard and it slammed on its hinges. Luke stared after her, knowing he'd gone too far, pushed too hard. But it had to be done. There was no other way. No matter the pain that pierced his soul, he could never have this woman he'd come to adore. He was poisonous. Toxic.

His father had called him worthless. Standing ramrod straight in dress whites, cap tucked officially beneath his arm. *"Worthless,"* he'd said.

And now Luke could add *liar* to the list of charges. His insides churned as the losses piled up. The reputation he'd worked so hard to create was crumbling like the rest of his life. But if the lie served its purpose, kept Claire and everyone else away from him, it was worth the sin.

And now, just like his parents, Claire was gone. On her way out of his life she'd even bought into the charge that he could be a thief. Had she ever truly believed he was completely innocent? Had standing up for him just been another pretty face she'd put on her life, another way of doing what she thought was the "right thing." Again the image of Lisa Evans surfaced. She'd taken everything of material value and walked away. The only difference in the two women was that Claire had walked away with his heart.

Now, there was nobody left to judge him, nobody to disapprove, nobody he could disappoint, and no reason to rush. Soon enough he'd be home to wander his little peanut field alone and ponder the woman who'd claimed to love Luke Dawson. Not wild and wildly rich Striker Dark, but scarred and imperfect Luke Dawson.

He glanced at the yellow roses thrown in the trash, the symbol of his beloved Claire, the Texas beauty. His gaze sought the crystal vase, empty and sad.

Just like his future.

The next morning Claire couldn't decide if Pastor Ken's study was cooler than usual or if the warmth had simply seeped from her soul. She'd always thought the emptiness she'd felt from her abuse and from watching her father's old sedan disappear around the corner were the worst life had to offer.

Yesterday she'd been proven wrong.

"I don't know what hurts more, the fact that he's wrong about himself or the possibility that he's right about me."

She'd gone through the hours since their confrontation on autopilot. Sitting behind her desk, working out a thousand small details. Everything from trailer rentals for the Sturgis trip to tickets for carnival rides. It kept her body occupied with work, but her mind was with Luke.

Recent memories flooded the organized, predictable spaces in her subconscious normally reserved for comforting numbers and reliable facts. Instead, her mind's eye suffered through snapshots of the man she loved in all his forms; a stranger on the bridge, a musical mentor on a lighted stage, a willing chaperone holding her hand and laughing at her childish screams, a tender protector who interceded for others.

Interceded for her.

But was he also a master at deception? A thief?

"Pastor Ken, doesn't it make you angry deep down that he lied to all of us?"

Ken's head popped up from where he'd been studying the screen of his laptop, a look of disbelief in his kind eyes.

"You're starting to sound like Moe Saunders. That's not really how you feel is it? Luke may have omitted the whole truth, but I don't know that he ever lied to any of us. Certainly not to me."

"But he let us defend him all this time not knowing who he really was."

"I've known since the day we handled that incident with Nicole Arnold showing interest in Zach's finger as a keepsake."

The room shifted, leaned off-kilter. Fatigue was getting to her. What had he said? *Ken had known?* He must have read her puzzled expression.

"Luke needed to get some things off his chest. His

feelings for you were at the top of the list and he thought I'd understand his fears more easily if I had the whole story. I don't think he'd shared it for a lot of years and I was honored to have him confide in me."

"Should you be telling me this?"

"Luke's made his peace with it. He told me yesterday morning when I picked him up at your place that he didn't care who knew now. It's only a matter of days before everything comes to light anyway."

She looked at the man she'd always respected, seeing him from a new perspective. Even knowing the worst, he hadn't been judgmental. He'd stood against his church council, determined to give Luke and the Sons the break they'd all deserved.

"What about Rambling Records? We still don't know if Luke's in the clear. You said yourself Luke wouldn't feel responsible for that money if he was innocent."

"I said he *shouldn't* feel responsible. Big difference, but considering what I've seen of Luke Dawson I'm not surprised that he's determined to make restitution."

"But Luke said—"

Ken waved away the thought. "Luke *wants* you to let him go. That's the only reason he told you that. Daniel says there's no evidence of any tie between Luke and Scott Rambling's shenanigans. I don't need to wait for the official report to know our boy's in the clear."

Claire's gut twisted. How could she have doubted Luke even for a moment? How could she have thrown such a hurtful accusation at a man who'd just said he loved her?

He'd even shared his heart with Ken.

"He told you he had feelings for me?" She tried to say it casually, but asking Ken for confirmation of another man's emotions was like passing a note in study hall.

Ken's smile was understanding. His knowing eyes squinted with kindness.

"It was much more than that, Claire. He was already falling in love with you and he was troubled about where it was headed. He was in tune to all your body language, knew there was heartbreak in your life and didn't want to add to it. He wanted me to pray with him about his past, about you. He's so afraid he'll blemish your reputation, undo all your hard work."

She stilled, her hand poised above the gold cross she'd been worrying constantly for the past thirty-six hours. For the first time since she'd stomped out of his apartment she began to consider Luke's feelings. From what she'd read on the Internet and seen in the cable spots, he'd had a much harder time of it than anything she'd experienced, since his actions had been judged in the media. Naturally he'd guard his privacy closely, just as she did.

And how many times had he told her and others that his work was more than a business? It was his mission, the way he gave back, showed his gratitude for God's goodness. And now he'd even admitted it was the work he did to earn forgiveness, to try to cleanse himself from the deeds of his youth. Was he really afraid the dirt in his life would make her dirty, too?

She understood that logic. Felt it herself at times.

"Let me show you something I keep handy." Ken interrupted her thoughts. He leaned down and tugged open his bottom desk drawer, rummaged beneath some papers, and handed a snapshot across the desk.

"Recognize anybody in that photo?"

Claire studied the group of scruffy haired college-age men in baseball caps and dark sunglasses. They puffed their chests out to display the crude slogans on their shirts. Arm in arm, they held beer cans aloft in a cocky salute. She raised her eyes to Ken for a clue.

"Just an average bunch of reprobates, huh?" he teased.

She shrugged, no idea where this was headed, and no energy to figure it out.

"Does this help?" He dragged a nearby Astros cap over his head, slipped on his sun shades and brandished his diet soda can.

"You?" She stared at the photo, amazed that her

pastor was once a rowdy young man. "This is *Ken Allen?*"

"I wonder the same thing every time I look at it," he chuckled. "But I keep it close to remind me that everybody has something in their past they might regret and they're entitled to keep that something private. It's the sum total of our life experiences that makes us who we are today.

"Claire, what you've been through has made you a survivor, determined never to be a victim again. Luke's no different. His past is what produced the strong, caring Christian man he is today. Give him a break, accept him as he is." Ken leaned forward and placed his warm hand over Claire's icy ones.

"And give yourself a break, too."

"Claire, that fella from *Today's Times* magazine is out here. You got a minute?"

Her head snapped up from the endless list that had occupied her days. With her mind so crowded with pain and worry, she hadn't given a thought for Arthur O'Malley since the night of the accident. If he was in Houston that couldn't be a good sign. Maybe the follow-up piece was back on again.

"Just what I need," she groaned into the speaker phone.

"I can tell him you're tied up but he already knows you're here because your car is out front."

"No, it's okay, Justin. Give me a couple of minutes and then tell him to come on back. Unfortunately, he knows the way."

She puffed out a sigh that blew her bangs off her lashes, a reminder that she was days overdue for her hair appointment with Manuel. Pulling open her pencil drawer, she reached for her spare cosmetic bag and hand mirror. She held the glass aloft and studied the reflection. Tired smudges marred the skin beneath her eyes, a host of zits threatened to emerge on her chin at any moment and the only lipstick she had left was on her teeth. A rueful smiled twisted her mouth, first over the pitiful picture she made and then at the silly thought of doing anything about it. She was working day and night and there was nothing wrong with looking the part. She shoved her supplies back in the drawer and pushed it shut. Arthur O'Malley had all the story he was going to get from her. If he'd unearthed information someplace else, she'd just trust God to use it for good.

"Knock, knock." O'Malley stood at her door, looking deceptively charming, polished and professional, an alligator briefcase in his hand.

She rose and noted the way her silk slacks bagged at the knees and her blouse sagged from the summer heat. So what?

She refused to give him a warm welcome. "What brings you back to Houston so soon?"

"The same thing that's got half the journalists in

the country in a stir. Striker Dark." O'Malley smiled, the Cheshire cat so sure he knew all.

"Oh." She motioned for him to take a seat and she sunk back into her leather chair.

"Not much surprises me these days, but I have to admit that visit from Dawson was a shocker. I'm guessing we can count on you to keep him from slipping back into oblivion."

"Not that it's any of your business, but my future has nothing to do with Luke."

"After what that guy did for you, you can't be serious." He squinted, eyeing her closely. "But you're looking fairly miserable right now, so maybe you are."

She shoved the bangs out of her eyes.

"Listen, this week has been one of the longest in my life and it's only Friday. I still have the weekend to get through."

"Sorry, I won't keep you much longer." He pulled a legal-size envelope from his briefcase and deposited it on her desk. "I just needed to drop off these drawings of the bike that you loaned me. Dawson's conditions required that I return them immediately and personally guarantee you the follow-up piece is permanently cancelled. In light of the recent developments, I'm sure you understand." He stood. "I'll be on my way. I've got a meeting with Dawson within the hour."

"Well, you've wasted your trip to Houston because he's already gone. He left without so much as a goodbye for the guys in the band."

"You really haven't spoken with him lately, have you?" O'Malley looked skeptical.

She shook her head.

"Dawson's still in town. I'm meeting with him at his apartment."

The urge to go to him was strong, but she and Luke had said all there was to say when they'd flung their hurtful words at one another. He wanted her to stay away, and she would.

O'Malley flicked back the cuff of his monogrammed dress shirt to check his gold watch, and then stood. "You want to join us?"

"No, thanks, I'm not sure I'd be welcome. Besides—" she swept an open palm above her cluttered desk "—I'm finishing up a couple of projects here. I have a mountain of work to wrap up in the next twenty-four hours."

She stood and reluctantly accepted the hand he offered. He held it, staring down at her.

"I was there, Claire. Early in my career I was one of the idiots who hounded Striker. I'm certain Luke recognized me that night I came to the church. That's why he was so rude to me. And I probably had it coming because I was one of the worst. We hunted him for amusement, to catch him already in trouble or to push him to the brink of it. The drugs made him easy prey. Guess I owe him an apology.

"He really must care for you. There's no other reason the man would subject himself to this. Whatever he might have done, forgive him. He's earned it."

O'Malley gave her hand a final squeeze and left to keep his appointment with the man she loved.

Loved, but could never have.

In the quiet of her office, she sat perfectly still and considered the events of the past week. Luke had sacrificed everything that was important to him in order to protect her. And she had to ask herself whether she'd have done the same for him? Exposed that darkest part of her life she worked diligently to keep buried in fathoms so deep the nightmares couldn't surface.

She'd seen his eyes brim with shame when he'd told her the truth. How much harder was it going to be for such a proud man to expose his sins before the media that had hunted him like an animal? The media that saw his story as nothing more than a marketing piece.

When this weekend was over she'd find Luke, tell him she understood, and ask for his forgiveness. And though it would be the hardest loss of her life, she'd say goodbye with a smile on her face to the man of her dreams who'd saved her from her nightmares.

Chapter Sixteen

⌒◝⌒

The Praise Productions trailer was loaded and the truck was packed and gassed up for the long ride home to Georgia. All he had left to do was swing by the kennel and pick up Freeway. But directions to the amphitheater on the seat beside Luke beckoned like a siren. He couldn't stay away. Not when he'd promised. Not after the long hours he'd invested in Eric, in all four boys and their support crew. Luke regretted that he wouldn't be personally involved in the recording but the least he could do was show up and cheer them on and then give each young man a personal goodbye.

Luke was only there for the kids. Yeah, right. Who was he fooling? Certainly not himself. He was there to find Claire, tell her the truth, that he'd never taken anything that wasn't his own because he knew the pain of being duped. He'd apologize for the cruel things he'd said to her, ask for her forgiveness and maybe get one final smile from her to ease the ache deep in his chest.

The pathway from the parking lot to the amphitheater was alive with sparkling lights and excited chatter. Luke fell in step with the throngs of visitors, now and then getting a wave from someone he recognized. Not knowing if he'd be a welcome sight picked at his insides, but the friendly smiles and occasional claps on the back told him folks either didn't know or didn't care about the recent revelations that had made him withdraw from the Abundant Harvest community.

As he wound his way up the path busy with pedestrian and golf cart traffic, he marveled at the festive surroundings. Contemporary praise music poured from speakers in the distance, calling the visitors to a celebration of their faith.

Luke drew closer to the center of the excitement, a crescendo of anticipation building inside him. He marveled at the quick work of what had to have been an army of volunteers to pull such an event together in a matter of days. So this was the surprise Claire was talking about when she said the church was helping somebody out of a tough spot. His gut twisted with sinful envy, knowing he'd never deserve such an outpouring of support.

He topped the hill and watched the activity in the man-made valley below with fascination. The open-air amphitheater was surrounded by sideshow-style games and activities. The little ones waited impatiently for their turn to defy gravity in the moon walk while the older kids battled against the clock in an inflatable obstacle course. The lights from carnival rides flashed in time with pulsing music and everywhere there was laughter and fun. Not something most folks would expect from a church function, but then this was not your grandma's church.

He wound his way through the quickly gathering crowd to where the professional crew at the side of the stage was testing the sound, preparing for the recording session that was only minutes away. He had to admit it would be a kick to work with a big organization like Battle of the Bands. The years of experience shared between the owners and their employees, and their goal of giving high school bands a leg up in the business, was an attractive proposition that had seeped into Luke's daydreams.

At least in what little space wasn't already occupied with equally absurd thoughts of a life with Claire.

"Luke! You're here!" Eric's voice cracked with excitement over the discovery. He bounded down the steps from the stage and into Luke's arms, as unconcerned for propriety as a small child whose only goal is to seek comfort from a loving parent. Luke's throat swelled with gratitude for the show of affection from the boy he'd come here to protect. The boy starved for fatherly love.

"Where else would I be?" Luke returned Eric's hug.

"Will you watch from backstage? We're ready but it would help to have you close by."

As they wove through the maze of equipment on the stage Luke's stomach muscles tightened at the anticipation of seeing his brown-eyed beauty again. But she was nowhere to be found.

"Where's Claire?" he asked, knowing Eric would see through any wasted efforts to beat around the bush. "I figured she'd be back here with you guys."

"We've already had our prayer time and she's gone out front to watch."

"Fifteen minutes!" the stage manager shouted.

The familiar warning rang in Luke's mind, his adrenaline surged in a second-nature reaction.

"Come on, let's go see the guys and get you ready for your big moment."

Ten minutes later with microphone in hand, Pastor Allen crossed the stage, ready for his duties as the evening's emcee.

"Welcome to the debut recording concert of the Harvest Sons!" He brought the audience to their feet with enthusiastic cheers for their hometown boys. "Thanks for coming on such short notice to be a part of this special evening." He spread his arms to indicate the size of the event. "All of this was pulled together by the hard working council of Abundant Harvest Church, led by our very own Claire Savage.

The proceeds from tonight will go to Praise Productions to help share in a recent effort to offset
some investment losses by sister churches in another state. This is our small way of thanking Luke
Dawson for the incredible work he's done with the
Harvest Sons."

Luke heard the announcement from his position
off-stage, deep in the curtains where only the band
could see him. The crowd shouted their approval,
music that fell sweet on Luke's ears. It was for Praise
Productions. For him. Undeserved, like every other
blessing in his life.

"Thank You, Father," Luke uttered, unable to
grasp the enormity of what these people had done
for him, what Claire had done for him in spite of his
cruel behavior.

Ken turned toward the spot where Luke was anchored and motioned for him to take a bow. The
band took the stage, stood behind their instruments
and applauded, refusing to stop until Luke made an
appearance.

Icy worry twisted inside as he edged out of his
hiding spot. For the first time in fifteen years the
people out front knew him for his true identity. As
a spotlight found him on the edge of the stage the
applause grew, accompanied by cheers of approval.
He gave a quick wave and ducked his head to turn
away.

That's when he saw her.

Claire stood near the front of the crowd, looking as young in her jeans and lightweight blue pullover as the kids who surrounded her. She waved and pointed to the soundboard at the edge of the stage where Dana was perched on a high stool beside the audio professionals, no doubt telling them how to do their jobs. Dana gave him a thumbs-up, confirmation the show was ready to go on. His gaze sought Claire's one last time before he drifted behind the curtain. In her eyes he saw only forgiveness. Only love.

Zach raised his drumsticks overhead.

"A one, two, three, four," he shouted as he tapped out the cadence, counting them into the first number. They opened with the song they'd done for the audition, one the Sons were sure of, one that was certain to keep the audience energized and on their feet. The pride Luke felt surpassed anything in his memory. He loved these boys, loved the woman out front more that his own life. How would he find the strength to drive away?

The big finish was coming. Eric mugged for the girls in the audience, striding to the front of the stage, breaking with the practiced choreography. He enjoyed the moment a little more than he should, an area where Luke had a lot of experience. The boy swung his arm wide, windmill-style, fanning the air close to his instrument.

Luke heard the loud twang and grimaced at the

pain Eric must have felt as his palm made contact with the tremolo bar on his guitar. Eric flinched but continued with his stage show and ended the song as planned. He turned away from the cheering crowd, blood trailing on the floor, dripping from his palm.

Luke met Eric halfway across the stage and applied pressure with a towel he'd grabbed. Ken took over, welcoming special guests, thanking the Battle of the Bands recording crew while Luke determined the extent of Eric's injury.

"Man, I hate to tell you this but it needs stitches."

"Just put a bandage on it for now and we'll go to the emergency room after the show."

"It can't wait that long. Look how it's bleeding." Luke exposed the wound briefly. "If you don't get this taken care of right away you could end up with permanent scarring, maybe even lose some feeling in your hand."

Eric's normally fair skin was becoming paler by the second. The possibility of missing his chance to record and letting his friends down was evident in his glistening eyes.

"There's always an EMT truck required at these things. Let's get you out to them. Those guys can have you stitched up and back on stage in no time."

"What'll the Sons do till then?"

"Just leave that to me."

Ken was beside them, taking control, shepherding Eric toward the stage exit. He looked over his shoulder at Luke.

"There's only one way to handle this, Luke. Do it." The pastor gave the order and Luke went into action before he had time to think it through, time to back out.

He crossed to Eric's position on stage and reached for the six-string Gibson Les Paul. The weight of the instrument at the end of his arm was a return to another life. The motion of raising the guitar to drop the shoulder strap over his head was magical, a movement he'd only performed in his dreams since the fire. His heart thumped a maddening beat against his ribs at the thought of making music again.

Recognizing what they were about to witness, the audience roared their approval. The rumble began.

"Striker! Striker! Striker!"

Claire held her breath afraid the moment would evaporate. Afraid the man she loved more than she thought possible would change his mind and disappear forever behind those dark curtains. The look in his eyes when he recognized what they chanted was sorrowful to watch. Would they never understand that was a lifetime ago, a lifetime Luke wanted to remain dead and buried?

Finally, she *fully* understood. His determination to leave wasn't to have things his way. It truly was to protect her from the masses calling his name, dragging him down, deep into the past he so desperately wanted to leave behind.

He turned his back to the crowd and signaled for Zach and Brian to join him at the keyboard with Chad. They pressed their heads together, spoke briefly and, if Claire was not mistaken, took a moment to pray. Luke fastened Eric's headset in placed and turned to the audience, motioning for quiet.

"Someday I'll find the words to thank you for all you've done for me these past weeks. But today is not about me. It's about the Harvest Sons and the message of their music. Eric's injured his hand but he'll be right as rain in a few minutes. Until he gets back we want to do a song for you to set the tone for the rest of the evening. We're going to slow things down for a few minutes, while we offer up our praise to the Savior who showed us an amazing love."

Luke fixed his eyes on hers and began to sing the words a cappella. Her breath caught in her throat at the honey-smooth richness of the voice he'd hidden until now. She had to look into those eyes, hear that voice for the rest of her days and she was prepared to do whatever it took to make that happen. She would not let him out of her life, no matter the cost, no matter the arrangement.

Never taking his gaze from hers, he deftly began to finger the strings and coax a perfectly pitched melody from the guitar as he sang the truth of the King who was forsaken.

Claire heard the swell of sound as the audience numbering close to two thousand picked up the refrain and sang along. Forgetting Striker Dark, knowing only that the man before them was sincere in his praise. Claire's voice blended with the others as best she could over the tightness in her throat. She felt tears spill over her lashes and trickle in streams down her cheeks, matching the same patterns she saw on Luke's face.

His heart was in his eyes as he sang, exposing his soul to her as hundreds looked on. The lazy smile that spread across his handsome face when the song ended was all the encouragement she needed. As an amphitheater full of Texans showed their approval, she squeezed through the tight throng, and dashed up the side steps past the grinning security guard.

Luke met her in the wings, his arms wide, hope shining in his green eyes. She pressed her face to his chest, clinging to him, her arms wrapped in a perfect fit around his waist.

"Forgive me?" she begged.

"Anything," he promised. "I adore you." He pressed soft kisses to the top of her head, his voice close to her ear. "God can do powerful work in us when we're weak so I should be a blank canvas for Him right now. I don't know what He has planned for the rest of my life but if you tell me it includes you, no matter where, I'll be a happy man."

Claire tilted her head to see into his eyes and

pulled him close for the tender kiss that was her answer. What had started out for both of them as painful, God had turned into good.

Together they would share an amazing life.

An amazing love.

* * * * *

Dear Reader,

Whether we choose them or they choose us, there are events in all of our lives that we'd like to change, run away from or forget entirely. The words that can't be reclaimed, the actions that can't be forgotten and the thoughts that can't be erased all linger in the form of guilt, mocking us and making us feel unworthy.

But the awesome thing about the boundless love of our God is that He forgives His truly repentant children and carries our sins as far away as the East is from the West. It's an act of love we humans can hardly comprehend, but we're told to mirror it in our daily lives. Forgiving others (especially when we think they don't deserve it!) allows us to accept the mercy the Father shows us (when we don't deserve it, either). Give it a try today. You'll be amazed at how much lighter your heart will feel tomorrow.

Please tell your friends about me and drop by for a visit at www.MaeNunn.com.

Until we meet again, let your light shine!

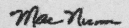

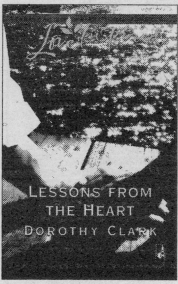

REQUEST YOUR FREE BOOKS!

2 FREE INSPIRATIONAL NOVELS
PLUS A
FREE
MYSTERY GIFT

Love Inspired.

YES! Please send me 2 FREE Love Inspired® novels and my FREE mystery gift. After receiving them, if I don't wish to receive any more books, I can return the shipping statement marked "cancel." If I don't cancel, I will receive 4 brand-new novels every month and be billed just $3.99 per book in the U.S., or $4.74 per book in Canada, plus 25¢ shipping and handling per book and applicable taxes, if any*. That's a savings of over 20% off the cover price! I understand that accepting the 2 free books and gift places me under no obligation to buy anything. I can always return a shipment and cancel at any time. Even if I never buy another book from Steeple Hill, the two free books and gift are mine to keep forever.

113 IDN D74R   313 IDN D743

Name	(PLEASE PRINT)

Address	Apt.

City	State/Prov.	Zip/Postal Code

Signature (if under 18, a parent or guardian must sign)

Order online at www.LoveInspiredBooks.com

Or mail to Steeple Hill Reader Service™:

IN U.S.A.	IN CANADA
3010 Walden Ave.	P.O. Box 609
P.O. Box 1867	Fort Erie, Ontario
Buffalo, NY 14240-1867	L2A 5X3

Not valid to current Love Inspired subscribers.

Want to try two free books from another series?
Call 1-800-873-8635 or visit www.morefreebooks.com

* Terms and prices subject to change without notice. NY residents add applicable sales tax. Canadian residents will be charged applicable provincial taxes and GST. This offer is limited to one order per household. All orders subject to approval. Credit or debit balances in a customer's account(s) may be offset by any other outstanding balance owed by or to the customer.

LIREG05

Love Inspired

A FAMILY FOREVER

BY

BRENDA COULTER

When her fiancé was killed, pregnant Shelby Franklin's dreams were shattered. Tucker Sharpe was there to pick up the pieces and offer her a solution: marry him for the baby's sake. But would love for an unborn child be enough to keep them together?

On sale March 2006

Available at your favorite retail outlet.

www.SteepleHill.com

Steeple Hill®

TITLES AVAILABLE NEXT MONTH

Don't miss these four stories in March

WHEN DREAMS COME TRUE by Margaret Daley
The Ladies of Sweetwater Lake

Zoey Witherspoon got the shock of her life when her estranged husband showed up on her doorstep more than two years after he was presumed dead in a plane crash. Though thrilled that he was alive, Zoey struggled with giving her heart back to a man who had the power to break it all over again.

LESSONS FROM THE HEART by Dorothy Clark

When newspaper reporter David Carlson and literacy worker Erin Kelly teamed up for a story, there was an instant spark. But when Erin discovered David's lack of faith, their budding romance fizzled. David tried to move on, but when faced with adversity, would he find himself drawn back to Erin and her God?

A MATCH MADE IN BLISS by Diann Walker
Part of the BLISS VILLAGE miniseries

Lauren Romey needed a vacation, so her friends suggested a bed-and-breakfast. But when she wound up at the wrong one, she found herself in the middle of a contest staged by Garrett Cantrell's daughters—"Win Daddy's Heart." Lauren wasn't looking for romance, but Garrett's love was an appealing prize.

A FAMILY FOREVER by Brenda Coulter

When her fiancé was killed, pregnant Shelby Franklin feared she wouldn't be able to provide for her unborn child. The marriage of convenience proffered by the man who would have been her brother-in-law was her only choice. Tucker Sharpe had promised to look after Shelby, and he's determined to help her find love again—with him.

LICNM0206